"Eliza, you are one of a kind. Do you realize that?"

Eliza adjusted her glasses as she studied his expression. "Is that a bad thing…or a *gut* thing?"

Gabriel flashed a smile. "I'm not sure yet. But I think it might be *gut*."

Eliza's face lit up. Gabriel had never seen her look so delighted. "Really?" she asked in a hesitant, disbelieving voice.

"You're interesting, Eliza. That's for certain. I can't figure you out like I can figure out other girls. Just when I think I get you, you surprise me. I like the challenge of figuring you out."

"You do?" Eliza looked like she might faint. Her face had lost its color and her lips trembled.

"Are you okay?" Gabriel asked.

"I just…no one's ever said anything like that about me before…" Eliza swallowed hard and shook her head. "Look at me, acting the fool." She held out a hand. "I ought to be helping you, not chitchatting like this while you're still on the ground."

Gabriel flashed a playful grin.

Eliza chuckled. It wasn't quite a laugh, but it was close.

After **Virginia Wise**'s oldest son left for college and her youngest son began high school, she finally had time to pursue her dream of writing novels. Virginia dusted off the keyboard she once used as a magazine editor and journalist to create a world that combines her love of romance, family and Plain living. Virginia loves to wander Lancaster County's Amish country to find inspiration for her next novel. While home in Northern Virginia, she enjoys painting, embroidery, taking long walks in the woods, and spending time with family, friends and her husband of almost twenty-five years.

Books by Virginia Wise

Love Inspired

Visit the Author Profile page at LoveInspired.com for more titles.

The Secret Amish Admirer

Virginia Wise

LOVE INSPIRED

INSPIRATIONAL ROMANCE

LOVE INSPIRED®

INSPIRATIONAL ROMANCE

Recycling programs
for this product may
not exist in your area.

ISBN-13: 978-1-335-58639-1

The Secret Amish Admirer

Love Inspired
22 Adelaide St. West, 41st Floor
Toronto, Ontario M5H 4E3, Canada
www.LoveInspired.com

Printed in U.S.A.

Favour is deceitful, and beauty is vain:
but a woman that feareth the Lord,
she shall be praised.
—*Proverbs* 31:30

To my Creative Women's Group—Michelle, Sara and Laura—for supporting one another's dreams. Distance can't separate friendship.

Chapter One

Eliza Zook woke up before the rest of the household and faced the day as she always did—with no-nonsense determination. She fumbled for the big, round glasses on the bedside table, and as she slid them on, the world came into focus. Beyond the quiet bedroom lay the village of Bluebird Hills, nestled in the green fields of Lancaster County. Eliza slipped out from under the handmade quilt and dropped her bare feet onto the hardwood floor with a quiet thump, shivered in the chill morning air, and lit the kerosene lantern. As the flame flickered to life, she suppressed a yawn and glanced at the battery-powered clock. One hour and forty-five minutes until she dropped off her niece and foster daughter, Priss, at the one-room schoolhouse.

Eliza dressed quickly, smoothed her brown hair into a neat bun and pinned on her prayer *kapp*, taking an extra minute to ensure everything was neatly in place. She made the bed, smoothing out every wrinkle and fluffing the pillow, before marching into the kitchen. Her mother, Lovina, stood at the sink, filling the kettle with water. "Running late, I see," she murmured. "School starts in an hour and a half."

Pulling back the yellow gingham curtain that covered the kitchen window, Eliza frowned. Darkness hung over the tidy front yard. An engine rumbled as a truck lumbered past the redbrick ranch house, headed toward Bluebird Hills' quaint little downtown a few blocks away. Eliza could barely make out the vehicle in the faint glow of moonlight. "The sun isn't up yet. I can't be that late."

Lovina shrugged and set the kettle onto the gas stove. "The early bird gets the worm, ain't so?"

Eliza's expression tightened as she nodded. Her mother had a gift for finding faults. Even so, Eliza made a mental note to wake up fifteen minutes earlier tomorrow. Surely her mother wouldn't find reason to criticize her then.

The rest of the morning continued in its usual orderly and predictable way. Eliza and Lovina sipped mugs of hot tea while preparing a breakfast of bacon, eggs, hash brown casserole, sourdough toast and sliced peaches. Six-year-old Priss trotted into the room, already dressed for school, as Eliza pulled the casserole from the oven. The room lit up with Priss's bright smile as she grabbed a slice of bacon with a pudgy hand and stuffed it into her mouth. "Sit down to eat," Eliza reminded her as she pinched a pink cheek and nodded toward the table. "And don't dawdle—you're running late again."

Priss's face fell as she dropped into a chair. "But I'm all ready. See, I even got my payer *kapp* on straight this time." Eliza saw the look on Priss's face and cringed inside. She had not meant to be critical. Somehow, in her rush to make everything go smoothly, she had hurt Priss's feelings. Again.

Like mother, like daughter.

Except Eliza wasn't anything like her mother. She glanced at the sixty-six-year-old woman standing at the stove, her apron and *kapp* perfectly starched and ironed, and not a hair out of place. While her petite frame and frown lines made her appear frail and elderly, she moved like a young woman, full of energy and vigor. Lovina Zook was a force to be reckoned with. She had a knack for getting things done—or as some people described it, bossing people around—and an air of confidence that Eliza simply didn't possess. She had tried. She'd tried so hard that it made her head ache. But somehow, she could never quite fill her mother's shoes.

Most of the time, Eliza felt that all she did was make things worse, even though she was trying to do the right thing. All she wanted was a well-run household that would satisfy her mother.

Or, if she was willing to admit it, maybe she actually wanted something much more than that: to be free from the pressure to be perfect.

Eliza sighed. "I'm sorry, Priss. I didn't mean…" Eliza frowned and cut her eyes to Lovina, then back to Priss. "I didn't mean to criticize you. You've done a great job getting ready this morning. I just don't want us to be late."

"You're always worried about being late, and we never are," Priss said between two big bites of hash brown casserole.

"Because I worry about it, I take action to make sure it doesn't happen," Eliza said.

Priss furrowed her brow as she chewed, then swallowed. "Seems like there're better things to worry about." Priss considered this for another moment, then straightened in her seat as her face lit up with an idea. "Or you could just stop worrying at all. I don't like it."

Eliza's chest constricted. It seemed like the harder she tried, the harder she failed. Worrying was just one more strike against her parenting. When her sister, Rebekah, had abandoned the Amish faith, she'd left her daughter, Priss, behind, and Eliza had raised the child as her own ever since. The entire community considered Eliza to be Priss' mother and the little girl always called her *Mamm,* instead of *Aenti.* Eliza knew Priss needed tenderness and understanding after suffering rejection from her biological mother, and Eliza tried hard to give her that. But Priss also needed a firm hand, or she might end up going astray just like Rebekah had. At least, that's what Lovina had warned. And Eliza was afraid Lovina had a point.

But one look at Priss's expression melted Eliza's heart. "You're right, Priss. I shouldn't worry. I should leave everything in *Gott's* hands."

Priss gave a satisfied nod as she picked up her last strip of bacon. "So you won't mind if we take the long way to school so we can pet the llamas behind the Yoder farm?"

Lovina shook her head as she began to clear the table.

Eliza sighed. "*Nee*. We still have to stay on schedule."

Priss groaned dramatically. "Schedules are so boring."

"Maybe," Eliza said. "But they keep everything running smoothly. A predictable life is a good life."

After a fifteen-minute buggy ride to the one-room schoolhouse, Eliza dropped Priss off according to schedule, then drove the buggy past a half-mile stretch of pastureland to the gift shop and farm stand where she worked. The little pink-and-white building with gingerbread trim looked like a Victorian dollhouse alongside the highway. Eliza passed the big hand-painted sign that read "Aunt Fannie's Amish Gifts" as she pulled into the gravel parking lot. Morning sunlight shone across the acres of green and brown fields beyond the farmyard and sparkled across a small pond. A windmill overlooking the water creaked as its metal blades turned lazily in the breeze.

Emerald, ruby and purple dresses hung on a clothesline behind a rambling white farmhouse where Levi and Katie Miller, the owners of the farm and gift shop, lived. A massive red barn stood in the background, surrounded by split rail fences, bales of hay and hens pecking at the dirt. Inside, Eliza could hear the low, muffled mooing of the dairy cows. A rooster crowed and a dog barked in the distance.

Eliza's stomach tightened when she caught sight of Gabriel King in the south pasture beyond the barn. From any distance, she knew that silhouette anywhere. He was tall and boyishly handsome, with well-developed muscles from working as a farmhand for the Millers. Her heart fluttered every time she looked at him. Especially when he flashed his signature mischievous grin.

Gabriel King was Eliza's one great weakness, and had been since the third grade when he'd first turned that roguish smile on her. Eliza knew he was bad news—it was common knowledge that he had a rebellious spirit and was taking too many liberties on his *rumspringa*, which he kept extending. People whispered that he didn't fit in on the Miller farm—or anywhere in Bluebird Hills. There was even talk that he might jump the fence and go *Englisch* one day. Not to mention that Gabriel would never be interested in Eliza.

He barely even noticed she existed. And why would he when he had plenty of pretty, popular girls running after him? Eliza was too plain and predictable to ever attract a fun-loving, good-looking boy like Gabriel.

Eliza watched Gabriel lead a large black horse named Thunder through the high grass, then turned away. She unhitched and stabled her buggy horse, Bunny, and hurried toward the shop's entrance to ensure everything was neat and tidy before it was time to open to customers.

A high-pitched whinny followed by a strangled shout grabbed Eliza's attention before she opened the gift shop door. She jerked around to face the noise, then squinted through the thick lenses of her glasses.

A jolt of panic raced through her.

Thunder ran wild through the south pasture, the rope trailing behind. Dust billowed up from the powerful hooves, but Eliza could still make out the shape of a man tangled in the rope, dragging behind the horse.

Eliza did not think or plan. She acted on instinct. Her heart crashed into her throat as her feet pounded across the farmyard, chickens scattering in her wake. She flew into the south pasture, gasping for breath as the enormous horse wheeled around and headed in her direction. Gabriel shouted a warning. The world shifted into slow motion as the panicked animal bore down on her, foaming with sweat, eyes wild and flashing white. Hoofbeats thundered across the packed earth like drumbeats that echoed in Eliza's chest. Her mouth went dry, and her body froze. Another few seconds and those sharp black hooves would trample her.

The world whizzed past in a blur as Gabriel made out a solitary figure planted in front of Thunder. He twisted his body, but the rope held fast around his leg. "Eliza!" he shouted. "Get out of the way! You're going to get yourself killed!" What was she thinking? Gabriel grimaced in pain as his body bounced and slammed against the earth. He yanked at the rope tangled around him, but the force of the running horse pulled it taut. It was hopeless.

Gabriel never thought very far ahead. He lived for the day, for the moment. At twenty-one years old, he was young enough for that luxury. He had all the time in the world to relax and enjoy a few wild years.

Until now. He could not believe it might end this way. What a stupid, careless way to go.

And now Eliza was going down with him, for no reason. He wished that guilt wouldn't be the last thing on his conscience. He had enough of it to wrestle with as it was.

"Eliza!" Gabriel shouted again. Dust filled his mouth as his shoulder skidded over a clump of dirt. "Get out of the way!"

She didn't move.

"Eliza!"

Eliza put out a hand and stared at the horse. Gabriel knew that everything was happening as quick as a heartbeat, but his senses had slowed, and he felt as though he were being dragged through water. The moment seemed to last forever as he watched Eliza hold that position, shoulders back, mouth set in a determined line.

"And just where do you think you're going?" she asked in her usual no-nonsense way, her tone firm but reassuring. "You can't keep running forever, so you may as well stop now." She stared the animal down with the same look she gave whispering children during church services. The horse snorted, jerked his head and slowed to an agitated prance. "That's right," Eliza said. "Go on and stop this nonsense before someone gets hurt."

The horse snorted again, then shuddered to

a stop, sides heaving. He lowered his head and breathed heavily, foamy sweat glistening along his flank. Eliza reached forward and cautiously grabbed hold of the rope. She patted his neck with her other hand and clucked her tongue. "Acting the fool like that. Could have gotten somebody killed."

"He doesn't understand, you know," Gabriel said from where he lay sprawled in the dirt. He pushed himself up, groaned and collapsed back to the ground.

"*Ach*, he understands well enough," Eliza said. "And he knows he ought to be ashamed of himself for running wild." As if on cue, the horse looked away and gave a mournful whinny.

"One of your looks is enough to scare anybody, Eliza."

"You're welcome," she said.

"*Danki*. Didn't mean to sound ungrateful. It's just… I've never seen anybody do that before."

"Stop a horse? It really isn't that big a deal."

"I mean I've never seen anyone stop a horse with a *look* before."

"Nonsense. He had already worn himself out. He was ready to stop."

She pushed her glasses up the bridge of her nose and stared down at him.

"You're mighty calm right now to have just put yourself in the path of a runaway horse," Gabriel said after a few beats. "Maybe a little *too* calm. Shouldn't you be crying or fainting or something?"

"It would pretty inconvenient if I collapsed, too, ain't so? I think one person laid out in the dirt is enough for today."

Gabriel flashed a weak smile. "You got me there. I guess this makes you a hero. What do you think of that?"

"Nonsense. I just did what anyone would do."

"You and I both know that's not true."

Eliza looked away as her cheeks flushed red.

"Why, Eliza Zook, did I just make you blush?"

Eliza's face swung back toward Gabriel. "You seem pretty calm yourself. Maybe you took a hit on the head. You probably shouldn't be smiling so much."

"Can't smile at the woman who rescued me?"

Eliza's expression of perplexed shock made Gabriel chuckle. "I've never seen that look on your face before, Eliza. Was it something I said?"

She blinked rapidly.

"Left you speechless, huh? I do have that effect on women, you know."

Eliza's shocked expression snapped into a frown. "That's quite enough out of you, Gabriel King. You must have a concussion to be carrying on so."

Gabriel shrugged and flashed a playful grin.

"Are you hurt, or are you just wallowing in the dirt for fun while you tease me?" Eliza asked.

Gabriel realized he was still lying on the ground while Eliza peered down at him, hands firmly planted on her hips. He lifted himself onto his elbows and glanced over his body. "Too much adrenaline to tell at the moment." He gave himself a quick pat down. "Everything seems intact." But when he touched his ankle, pain shot up his leg and he winced.

Eliza shook her head. "Best get you to a doctor."

Gabriel frowned. "Hate to make a fuss."

Eliza raised an eyebrow.

"*Oll recht*," Gabriel muttered before dropping his head back to the ground and closing his eyes. "You win."

* * *

Eliza watched the ambulance back out of the gravel driveway and onto the highway. The lights flashed blue and red, but the siren remained silent as the vehicle zipped away. Thankfully, Gabriel was not so badly injured that the paramedics had to rush him to the hospital. In fact, he had been well enough to make fun of her. She had always suspected that he smiled and joked to cover up how he really felt. He had probably been hurting badly. He probably still was.

The thought made her chest tighten. She kept her eyes on the back of the ambulance until it disappeared beyond a distant hill and she was left alone in the empty farmyard. Eliza wanted to be in the ambulance with Gabriel. She wanted it so badly it made her feel sick and hollow inside.

Eliza let out a long, shuddering breath. She looked down at her clasped hands and realized she was shaking. In that terrible moment, when the horse had charged toward her, her entire focus had been on saving Gabriel. Nothing else had mattered. But now that Gabriel was safe, all the emotion she had pushed aside was rushing back.

Gabriel could have been killed. They both could have been killed.

"Thank you, *Gott*, for protecting us and using me to help Gabriel," Eliza whispered. She closed her eyes, let the relief sweep through her; then she opened her eyes and forced herself to walk toward the gift shop. There was no use standing in the driveway, feeling upset. That wouldn't do anybody any good. No, she may as well get back to work. That was why the Millers had left her behind. Someone had to mind the shop, and it made sense that it should be her. Levi wasn't just Gabriel's boss; he was a longtime family friend. And even though Katie had only known Gabriel's family since she moved to Bluebird Hills the previous year, she would still feel responsible. She and Levi were only in their late twenties, but took their work seriously and played an important role in the lives of their employees and neighbors.

Eliza, on the other hand, was nobody to Gabriel. Just an awkward woman with bony knees and elbows, mousy brown hair, and big round glasses. He wouldn't even notice that she had been left behind. He would probably forget that he had called her a hero.

But she would never, ever forget. That was

certain sure. And she would never let go of the wild hope that someday she could win his heart—no matter how impossible that seemed, and no matter how often she had been warned against his rebellious ways.

Chapter Two

The Millers' buggy pulled into Gabriel's yard and shuddered to a stop in front of the small, white clapboard house he shared with his aunt Mary, his father's much younger sister. The jolting motion shot pain up his bandaged ankle. He grimaced and reached for the crutches one of the nurses at the emergency room had given him. As he scooted to the edge of the buggy's bench seat, the front door of the house flew open and Aunt Mary rushed out, drying her hands on her apron. "What's happened?" she asked as she hurried toward them, staring at the white gauze wrapped around Gabriel's head. She didn't seem to notice the dusting of flour on her cheek or the loose strand of dark brown hair that had escaped her prayer *kapp*.

"He's okay," Levi said as he hopped out

of the driver's seat. Katie followed close behind. "There was an accident this morning," she said. "He's got a bad sprain and some cuts and bruises but nothing worse. He had to have a few stitches here and there. And he'll have to stay off that foot for a while."

"We called from the hospital and left a message at your phone shanty," Levi added quickly. "I'm sorry we didn't have time to get word to you in person. They treated and released him pretty quickly."

Mary looked at Gabriel with concern in her eyes. "Did anyone contact your father?"

His mouth tightened and he shook his head. "No need."

Mary frowned and reached for Gabriel's arm to help him out of the buggy.

"I can manage," he said and waved her away.

Her frown deepened but she stepped back. "What happened?"

"I was working with that new horse, Thunder. The one Levi bought at the auction a couple weeks ago."

"Did he throw you?" Mary asked. Her hand fluttered toward Gabriel as he lowered himself from the buggy, but she held back when he managed to land on his good leg and balance on his own.

"Nee." Gabriel looked away. He hated to admit how careless he'd been. He had struggled to get along with his father after his mother died seven years ago, so he'd moved in with his Aunt Mary, who was only thirteen years older than him. He had been trying to prove that he wasn't the failure his father thought he was ever since. "He got spooked and dragged me. Got tangled in the lead somehow. I should have been more careful."

Mary sucked in her breath through her teeth. "You could have been killed."

"Ya," Gabriel said as casually as he could manage. "That's what everyone keeps telling me."

Mary stared at Gabriel until he raised his eyes to hers.

"What would we do without you?" she asked.

Gabriel shot her a casual grin and shrugged. "Worry a lot less," he said.

"That is not funny, Gabriel King," Mary said. "Now, go on inside and put that foot up." She turned to Levi and Katie. "Won't you *kumme* in for a visit? I was just pulling a shoofly pie from the oven when I saw you through the window." She shook her head. "Scared me certain sure to see Gabriel looking so banged up." Mary's hand went to the loose strand of hair that had fallen from her *kapp*, and she quickly tucked it back into place.

"You ruined your good stockings," Gabriel said as he hobbled past Mary on his way toward the front door.

She looked down and laughed. "*Ach*, I was so upset when I saw that bandage on your head that I didn't take the time to put on my shoes." She lifted a foot and checked the sole of her black stocking. "Coated in mud, ain't so?"

Gabriel didn't say anything, but his heart warmed at the thought that Aunt Mary cared enough to dash outside in her stocking feet without even thinking about it. He wondered what his father's reaction would have been had he been there. He would have probably grunted, scolded him for being foolish enough to get dragged behind a horse and then gone back to whatever he had been doing. He certainly would not have run outside to check on him.

"Nothing a little soap and water can't get out," Mary said cheerfully as she shooed everyone inside.

After Mary changed her stockings and Levi tended to his buggy horse, they all sat down in the living room for a thick slice of warm pie. Mary insisted that Gabriel take the upholstered armchair, while the others sat in the wooden rockers. Gabriel's ankle throbbed as he shifted in his seat, trying to get comfortable. Despite the pain, the quiet, familiar living room made him feel a bit better. The small space was sparsely furnished, but Mary's braided-rag rug, knitted blankets and crocheted cushion covers made the space feel warm and homey. The tall, clunky propane lamp stood in the corner, and Mary's worn Bible lay atop a wooden end table dented with old nicks and scratches.

Gabriel wondered what it would be like to venture out from Mary's home. He had dreamed about escaping the rigid rules of his community for so long; but sitting there, getting fussed over by his friends and family, made him wonder if he might miss some aspects of the Amish life after all. The *Englisch* world would be mighty different, that was for sure and certain. And he would be facing it alone.

"You sure you didn't get a concussion?" Mary asked.

"What?" Gabriel said after he realized she was addressing him.

"You're staring off into space."

"*Ach*, I was just thinking."

"More evidence that something's not right," Mary said with a wink and a chuckle.

Katie and Levi laughed. "I sure am thankful we can laugh about this," Levi said. "If it hadn't been for Eliza—"

"Eliza Zook?" Mary asked with a perplexed expression on her face.

"*Ya.* She's the one who stopped Thunder."

"She saved my life," Gabriel added quietly.

"The Eliza Zook that works at the gift shop?"

"*Ya,*" Levi and Katie said in unison.

"But…" Mary sat back in her chair and glanced from one to the other.

"It's unexpected for certain sure," Gabriel said and told her the story.

Mary shook her head. "I never would have thought she had it in her."

Gabriel shrugged, then stuffed a big bite of shoofly pie into his mouth. He didn't think badly of Eliza. In fact, he hadn't ever thought about her enough to form an opinion one way or another. After working in the gift shop since she graduated from the one room schoolhouse down the road, she was a fixture on the Miller farm that had always been there, as unchanging and reliable as the furniture. But in all the years he had known her, she had barely spoken to him, so he had always assumed she was a bit standoffish and judgmental. After all, he did have a reputation for bending the rules, while she had a reputation as a stickler for them.

"She took on raising Priss when Rebekah left," Katie added. "That can't have been easy. She's done a *gut* job as a single mom, especially being so young herself."

"*Ya*, that's true," Mary said. "Such a sad thing. I don't think Lovina's ever been the same since losing her daughter. It made her…" Mary frowned and looked down at her plate. "*Ach*, I didn't mean to gossip. Please, forget I said anything."

Gabriel studied Mary's contrite face. She was nothing like her older brother—his father—who didn't have a problem saying harsh words about anybody. He claimed it was his right to point out another's faults in order to keep them on the straight and narrow. Gabriel knew there was a kernel of truth in that, but his *dat* pushed the concept too far to be reasonable or defensible. Gabriel almost let Mary's comment go, but he couldn't stop himself. "Lovina hasn't lost her daughter," he said.

"She's gone," Mary said as the crinkle in her forehead deepened. "Lovina will never see her again."

"It doesn't have to be that way," Gabriel said. "Rebekah isn't dead."

Katie and Levi exchanged a quick, concerned glance with each other. Levi nodded and stood up. "We best be getting back to the farm. Still have chores to do."

Katie followed Levi's lead and rose from her chair. "Thank you, Mary. The pie was delicious. And, Gabriel, we'll keep you in our prayers."

Gabriel wondered if she was alluding to more than just his sprained ankle. It was obvious that the comment he'd made about Rebekah's shunning had made them all uncomfortable.

"Oh," Katie added, "I forgot to tell you that Levi and I talked it over while you were with the doctor, and we want you to help out in the shop until you're better. You can't work the farm on that ankle."

Gabriel's stomach sank. "The shop?"

"*Ya*. Eliza will give you something to do that doesn't require manual labor."

"*Ach*, I can manage the farm—"

"Not a chance," Levi said. "I've already made the decision. You have to take it easy for a while."

Gabriel let out a long breath of air. He knew he should be thankful that the Millers were giving him an opportunity to keep earning a paycheck while he was temporarily injured, but being cooped up in the shop all day with Eliza Zook sounded like a terrible idea. She probably wouldn't speak to him, and if she did, it would only be to tell him he had broken some rule. That was the type of person she was. And, like his father, she would probably think she was doing him a favor.

"I know you're not used to doing paperwork or interacting with customers—but don't worry, you'll do great," Katie said.

Gabriel forced a smile. Better to let her think that was what was bothering him. After all, Eliza had just saved him. He shouldn't be so negative about her, even if she was difficult to deal with sometimes. "*Danki*, Katie. I'm sure it'll go fine."

As soon as the Millers finished their goodbyes and the door closed behind them, Mary turned to him with a severe expression. "Gabriel, you really have to stop this."

"Stop what?"

Mary put her hands on her hips. "They couldn't get out of here fast enough after you started talking about Rebekah Zook."

He put out his hands, palms up. "I only told the truth. She isn't dead, even if everyone acts like she is."

"It isn't that simple, and you know it."

"It could be. We don't have to make it so complicated."

"We keep the *Ordnung* for a reason. You can't go around questioning our ways. What will *gut* people like the Millers think? Don't you want to keep your job? And what about the rest of the community? Do you want this kind of talk to get around?"

"I guess they can think whatever they want about me. It won't change anything."

"It might! You have to protect your reputation. Don't you want to find a *gut* woman and settle down? What about your future?"

Gabriel closed his eyes and rubbed his temples. "We've had this conversation before, *Aenti* Mary."

"And one day I hope to finally get through to you."

"I'm just not sure I'm cut out for this life. I love you and I love..." He tried to gather his thoughts. "...A lot of things about being Amish. But I can't take all these rules. Sometimes I think I'll just walk away one day and never—"

Mary's face crumpled. "Gabriel, please. You don't know what you're saying."

"The problem is that I do," Gabriel said evenly.

Mary stared at him for a few beats, then

forced a smile. "How about a nice cup of hot cocoa? That's what you need right now."

Gabriel knew Mary couldn't handle the thought of him leaving the Amish, but he wished he could talk to her about it. Sometimes he felt so alone, even while surrounded by people. Gabriel sighed, then nodded. "Hot cocoa sounds great. *Danki.*" He would have to continue to keep his feelings to himself. Maybe one day he would meet an *Englisch* girl he could open up to. Until then, he was on his own to work through the feelings that tore him apart inside. Because no one who was Amish would ever understand him. That was for certain sure.

The next morning Eliza was straightening a display of homemade peach preserves when the bell above the door rang, and her attention shot to the entrance. Gabriel hobbled into the shop on crutches. Her heart fluttered at the sight of his handsome, boyish features. She tried not to stare at his adorably disheveled hair or the cute sprinkle of freckles across his nose.

"Looks like you're stuck with me," Gabriel said.

Eliza frowned. She didn't understand what he meant.

"Katie didn't tell you?" he asked.

"*Ach*, she's been busy helping Levi with a calving."

Gabriel slowly made his way around the back of the counter, then settled into a wooden chair. "They want me to work in the shop until my ankle gets better."

Eliza's stomach shot into her throat. Gabriel would be in the shop with her every day for the next few weeks! It felt like the best thing—and the scariest thing—that had ever happened to her. She stared at him for a moment as she tried to gather her thoughts and slow her heart rate. This was a dream come true while simultaneously being a nightmare. She would get to see Gabriel, but she would also have to make conversation with him. What would she say? How would she come across?

Uptight and unlikable, for certain sure. There was no way around it. She had no idea how to relax around Gabriel, much less impress him.

Gabriel stretched his injured leg in front of him and grimaced.

"Hold on," Eliza said. She hurried to the back of the shop, grabbed an empty wooden crate, made a beeline back to Gabriel and set the crate onto the floor beside his foot. "Here. You need to keep that foot elevated."

"Danki." Gabriel propped his foot up on the crate. Eliza noticed that his mouth tightened in pain at the movement, but he didn't complain. She had always liked that about him. Hidden beneath all his jokes and antics, he had a stoic, uncomplaining nature that showed an inner strength.

Eliza hovered over Gabriel, trying to think of what to say. "I've been worried about you," she said after a long silence. She regretted the words as soon as they left her mouth. "I mean, I wasn't worried—that is to say, I wasn't *thinking* about you. I just wondered…" She felt her cheeks flush and shook her head. "*Ach*, never mind. This floor won't sweep itself. I best get to work." She abruptly turned away from him and grabbed the broom. *He's laughing at me right now*, she thought. *He's thinking about how awkward I am. And, worst of all, he knows I was thinking about him!* Eliza could not bear the feeling of his eyes on her back, so she rushed to hide behind the nearest display shelf.

Eliza tried to forget about Gabriel as she attacked the floor with the straw broom, but her mind was stuck on him. She listened intently to every sound he made—the whisper of his bandage against the crate, his quiet humming and the drum of his fingers against the countertop. She wondered how long she could hide behind the shelves before it would be obvious she was avoiding him.

"Katie said there'd be some work for me to do here," Gabriel finally said, loudly enough for his voice to carry across the shop.

"Okay," Eliza managed to reply. She wasn't sure what else to say.

After a pause, Gabriel added, "Aren't you going to show me what to do?"

"*Ach*, of course," Eliza said. What had she been thinking, hiding from him like a flustered child when she was supposed to be helping? In her agitation, she dropped the broom, and the wooden handle clattered against the floor. She exhaled through her teeth, picked it up and marched over to Gabriel. "But, uh, I don't know what you can do."

Gabriel shrugged. "I'm not *gut* for much, huh?"

Eliza frowned. "That's not what I meant."

"I know, Eliza. I was joking."

Eliza swallowed hard. "Oh. Right. I thought that you thought that I thought that you're not capable, but I actually think—" She cut herself off and shook her head. "I'm not making any sense, am I?"

Gabriel grinned. *"Nee."*

"Never mind." Eliza wanted to run away as fast as possible. "Just sit here and wait for a customer. When someone makes a purchase, you can ring them up." Eliza fled to the other end of the shop before Gabriel could ask any questions. She heard his chair scrape across the worn wooden floorboards as he repositioned himself behind the register to wait.

Eliza spent a long time organizing the Mason jars of canned vegetables, then moved on to rearrange a display of faceless Amish dolls wearing purple cape dresses. She stepped outside to check on the bins of freshly picked spring vegetables on the porch before heading to the back of the shop. Twenty minutes crept past, then an hour. After that, she couldn't hide any longer. Every shelf had been dusted and straightened twice.

A customer wandered into the shop just in time to save Eliza from having to face Gabriel. "Hello!" Eliza shouted across the shop a little too enthusiastically. "How can I help you?" An *Englischer* wearing black yoga pants and a yellow T-shirt strode toward the canned-goods aisle without looking at Eliza. Eliza was used to being overlooked, so it didn't bother her. "These are all homemade?" the woman asked as she ran a manicured fingernail across the handwritten labels.

"*Ya.* And a lot of the ingredients are fresh-picked from this farm."

"Hmm," the woman murmured as she selected a glass jar of pickled beets and a jar of sauerkraut. She made a beeline for the counter and set the jars down beside the register. Eliza eased closer to watch Gabriel pick up each jar, squint at the label and then study the cash register buttons. The *Englisch* woman sighed and checked her watch. Gabriel frowned and pushed a button on the register. He looked back at the jar of pickled beets, then hit another button. "Um, sorry…" He scratched his head and glanced over at Eliza.

"Here," the woman said and handed Gabriel her card. He took it and stared at it.

The woman sighed again. "Aren't you going to run it?"

"Run it? *Ya.* That's exactly what I'm going to do."

Eliza hurried over to the register. She should never have left Gabriel so unprepared. It was her fault that he didn't know how to check out a customer. "It's simple," Eliza said as she slipped in front of the register. She pushed a few buttons on the register, ran the card and handed it back to the woman. "Sorry for the delay. He doesn't work here."

Gabriel raised his eyebrows at Eliza but said nothing.

"Then why is he here?" the woman asked.

"Because there's nowhere else for him to go." Eliza flinched inside. That hadn't come out quite like she meant it, but it was the truth. Eliza turned to Gabriel. "Bag her items."

"Right," he said in a flat tone. He grabbed a brown paper bag from the top of the stack beside the register, slid the jars inside and passed the parcel to the woman. "Have a nice day," he muttered.

The woman walked away without responding.

Gabriel waited for the door to shut, leaving them alone in the shop, then turned to look up at Eliza from his chair. "I didn't ask to be here, you know."

Eliza looked down at her hands. "*Ya*, I know."

"Let's just try and make the best of it," Gabriel said.

Eliza nodded.

He gave her a look that she couldn't quite interpret, but she was sure it wasn't good. She had obviously offended him, which was not a surprise. It seemed like the only time people noticed her was when she rubbed them the wrong way. "Here, this is all you have to do." Eliza's hands flew over the buttons on the cash register, the machine dinged and the cash drawer flew open. "See, it's simple."

"Well, *ya*, it is now that you've bothered to show me."

Eliza pushed her glasses up her nose with a slender forefinger. "You're right. I should have shown you."

"And you just slide the card through this thing?" Gabriel asked. His hand reached for the credit card scanner at the same time as Eliza, and their fingers brushed one another. Heat flashed up Eliza's arm. She had never actually touched Gabriel before—not in all the years she'd pined away for him. Her throat went dry and her knees felt watery. Eliza cringed and turned away. What a *narrisch* girl she was! It was ridiculous to have such foolish feelings for a man who would never think twice about her.

Eliza looked over at Gabriel and saw he was studying her with an odd expression. Her stomach clenched. "I…uh… I'm sorry, what were we talking about?"

"The credit card scanner."

"*Ya.* Of course. Um, it's all self-explanatory." She gave a quick demonstration and noticed her hands were shaking. *Get ahold of yourself, Eliza Zook. You know better than to get carried away by emotion.* Eliza looked over at Gabriel. He was watching her instead of the scanner.

"You okay?" Gabriel asked.

"Why wouldn't I be okay?" Eliza retorted with more edge to her tone than she meant.

Gabriel puffed out his cheeks and let the air out slowly. "Forget I asked," he said. "Matter of fact, just forget I'm here." And with that, he leaned back in his chair, pushed his straw hat over his face and closed his eyes.

He's going to take a nap right here in the shop! And he's obviously doing it so he doesn't have to talk to me anymore. Eliza was irritated and hurt, but she was also taken in by how cute he looked in that moment, which made her even more irritated. She stared at him for a few beats as he lounged in the chair—with that adorable, contented look on his face—then spun on her heels and stalked away.

Chapter Three

Gabriel knew Eliza disapproved of him, but this was getting ridiculous. She barely spoke to him all day and refused to show him how to do any of the jobs around the shop. When she finally did, she physically recoiled when their hands accidently brushed. He actually saw her flinch. He wanted to tell her that rebellion wasn't catching, so she didn't have to worry. But instead he had just stared at her in shock. She really must think he was a terrible person.

He couldn't completely blame her. Everyone knew that he had always pushed the limits of the *Ordnung*, and now that he was on his *rumspringa*, he flat out broke them. Eliza had seen his laptop and cell phone and had surely heard the rumors that he was considering leaving the Amish. It might have even gotten back to her that he had questioned Rebekah Zook's shunning.

But still. Eliza didn't have to be so obvious in her disapproval. As much as he hated to admit it, her judgment stung. It always had. She had been perfect since they were in grade school together. He had not paid much attention to her, except to notice that she never got in trouble and never made any mistakes. She was fastidious and careful in everything she did. Even as a young girl, she had managed to keep her apron neat and clean when the other girls dirtied theirs during recess. She always knew the answers when the teacher called on her, and she never forgot her homework. She seemed more like a character in a novel than a real person. How could anyone be that good?

Gabriel, on the other hand, had always been in trouble at school. So much so that his father expected it and was always ready with some harsh discipline. After a while, Gabriel acted out because it was expected. It had become part of his identity. And it was the only way he got attention. His father never noticed him when he was *gut*, but he sure did when he was bad. Eventually, Gabriel didn't know how to stop acting out anymore. So he just went with it. He also learned to make people laugh. That usually got him out of trouble. People seemed to forget they were upset with him if he lifted their spirits with a good chuckle.

But Gabriel's jokes never worked with Eliza the Perfect. She would just stare at him through those big, round glasses like she was looking down at a toad. Today had gone exactly as he had expected. And after she had judged and avoided him all morning, he finally gave up and tuned her out. Napping on the job was just one more strike against him, but he had already given up. Next time he would bring the woodcarving he had been working on with him. Whittling was one of his favorite ways to pass the time.

Six o'clock couldn't come fast enough. When it finally did, Gabriel grabbed his crutches and swept out of the shop without a word. Eliza would be glad to be rid of him, that was for certain sure. He hobbled down the front steps and onto the gravel parking lot, where one of his crutches slid out from under him. He jerked forward, barely keeping hold of his crutches before catching his balance. Gabriel frowned and dug his right crutch more firmly into the gravel. He glanced back at the shop and saw Eliza's face staring at him through the window.

Her frown matched his own. She flipped the sign from "Open" to "Closed" and pushed open the door without taking her eyes off of him.

Gabriel cringed. The last thing he needed was for Eliza to see his incompetence. He turned away and focused on keeping his balance as he hurried toward his buggy. Gravel crunched and rolled beneath his good foot. He knew he ought to slow down but refused. He managed until he was just an arm's length from the buggy, when his right crutch hit a pothole and he jolted to the left, lost his balance, and toppled to the ground before he could register what was happening. Pain exploded in his ankle and shot up his leg. He groaned and rolled his weight off the injury, palms stinging from where he had landed on them. Gabriel ignored the pain and tried to push himself off the gravel, but each stone dug into his flesh. He grunted and tried again.

"That's quite enough," a stern, determined voice said from above him.

Gabriel flinched. He knew the voice without having to look up. "I've got this, Eliza," he said. "You can go on home. Don't worry about me."

"Don't be ridiculous. I'm not going to leave you wallowing on the ground like a pig."

"Like a pig!" Gabriel felt a flash of irritation but realized he must look pretty silly and couldn't stop himself from laughing a little. He glanced up and shrugged. "Okay, maybe you're right."

Eliza wasn't laughing with him. Instead she looked slightly perplexed. "Of course I'm right. I wouldn't have said it if I weren't. You need help and you ought to accept it."

Gabriel shook his head. "Eliza, you are one of a kind. Do you realize that?"

Eliza adjusted her glasses as she studied his expression. "Is that a bad thing...or a *gut* thing?"

Gabriel flashed a smile. "I'm not sure yet. But I think it might be *gut*."

Eliza's face lit up. Gabriel had never seen her look so delighted. "Really?" she asked in a hesitant, disbelieving voice.

"You're interesting, Eliza. That's for certain sure. I can't figure you out like I can other girls. Just when I think I get you, you surprise me. I like the challenge of that."

"You do?" Eliza looked like she might faint. Her face had lost its color, and her lips trembled.

"Are you okay?" Gabriel asked.

"I just... No one's ever said anything like

that about me before…" Eliza swallowed hard and shook her head. "Look at me, acting the fool." She held out a hand. "I ought to be helping you, not chitchatting like this while you're still on the ground."

"*Wallowing* on the ground, you mean." Gabriel flashed a playful grin.

Eliza chuckled. It wasn't quite a laugh, but it was close. "*Ya.* Wallowing." She smiled and put out a hand for him.

"Why, Eliza Zook, I believe that's the first time you've ever liked one of my jokes."

Eliza looked away. "*Ach*, I don't know about that."

Gabriel raised his eyebrows. "You never smiled at them before."

Eliza looked like she might reply, but she hesitated, then shook her head. "Do you want help up or not?"

"I suppose I could use it."

Eliza sucked in her breath through her teeth when Gabriel lifted his hand to hers. "You've cut your palms."

"*Ach*, sorry, didn't realize I was bleeding. Guess I went down pretty hard."

"*Nee*, I didn't mean for you to apologize. I meant…" Eliza frowned as she stumbled over her words. She leaned closer, grasped him by the wrists and pulled. He used her for balance to leverage himself off the ground. But she didn't release him in time, and he stumbled forward as he stood, landing solidly in her arms.

Eliza gasped and jolted backward as if she'd been struck.

Gabriel felt a surge of shame. She obviously didn't want him to touch her. And why should she? She was far too good for him.

"I'm sorry!" they both shouted in unison. Gabriel stumbled backward and lost his balance. Her hands shot forward, grabbed his upper arms and steadied him. Their eyes met for a moment as she held him. A sensation rippled through Gabriel that he had never known before. He felt seen by Eliza, as if she was peering through his eyes, into the deepest part of him, where no one else had ever ventured. They held eye contact for a long, strange moment until Eliza dropped her hands from his biceps and pulled away from him.

Neither spoke for a moment, and Gabriel wondered if Eliza had experienced that same bizarre feeling he had. Then Eliza smoothed her apron, cleared her throat and said in a shaky voice, "I'll get something for those cuts. Then I'll hitch up Comet for you." She strode away without looking back. Gabriel noticed that she had called his horse by name. It seemed Eliza noticed more about him than she let on. Was there more to her than that distant, hard-as-stone persona she displayed?

Eliza felt like she might explode. Was it possible to feel an emotion this intense and survive? Her heart pounded in her throat, and her stomach felt like it had dropped to her toes. Gabriel had fallen into her arms. For one glorious moment, they had actually held each other.

And then he had stared into her eyes and seen her. Really *seen* her. He didn't tell her she was too prissy or too bossy or too perfect. He hadn't said anything at all. Had he been as frozen as she had been in that moment? Had he felt that same wonderful, terrifying rush when their eyes met that she had felt? She was sure he had. They had *connected*. She knew it. *Sensed* it.

But as she thought about it, she began to doubt. It had happened so fast, even though it felt like it had lasted forever. She must have imagined the connection. Because Gabriel King would never feel anything for her. Sure, he had said that she was interesting—and she would live off that compliment for years to come—but that didn't mean he *liked* her. It just meant he didn't hate her. She was probably interesting *to* him, like a zoo specimen. There was no way he saw her like a woman. No one saw her that way. They saw her as Lovina's daughter, as a hard worker, as a rule keeper. Not as a woman with her own personality waiting to be unveiled…

Eliza strode more forcefully toward the farmhouse. She had to put these *narrisch* thoughts out of her mind. Allowing herself to hope or dream would only lead to heartache. She must be out of her mind to indulge in such ideas! She had to accept that she would always be a nobody to Gabriel King.

Eliza wanted to look back toward him, but she forced herself to keep her attention straight ahead. She wondered if he was watching her. Of course he wasn't, but she couldn't help but hope. She hesitated, then allowed one quick peek over her shoulder.

Gabriel King *was* looking at her! She thought she might die, right there in the farmyard, beside the chicken coop. She jerked her face back toward the farmhouse and tried to calm her beating heart. Hope surged through her.

Until she wondered what he had been thinking as he stared at her. Maybe he was staring because he was trying to figure out what was wrong with her, why she was so weird…

Eliza hurried up the back steps, flung open the kitchen door and burst inside. Katie jumped and spun around from where she stood in front of the propane-powered refrigerator. "*Ach*, you startled me!"

"Sorry. I thought you were still in the barn, helping with the calving."

"I just came in for a few minutes to fix Simon something to eat."

"Hi, Eliza," Simon said from his seat at the kitchen table. A coloring book with a picture of a frog lay open in front of him. He looked at Eliza with solemn eyes—which appeared big and round through his thick glasses—then selected a green crayon and went back to coloring. Eliza had always liked Levi's son, who had recently become Katie's stepson. His serious, studious nature set him apart from the other children his age and he needed thick glasses, just like Eliza.

"I found a new salamander," Simon said without looking back up. He was busy concentrating on staying in the lines. "He's very cute. I'm sure you'll like him. Want to *kumme* up to my room and meet him?" Simon was always collecting reptiles and amphibians.

"I'd love to, but I don't have time right now," Eliza said. "Gabriel's cut himself, and I need to get some antiseptic for him."

"I'll get that for you," Katie said as she turned toward a kitchen cabinet. "What happened?"

"He fell on the gravel."

"Ouch. Poor guy. Do you want me to take care of it?"

"No!" Eliza said a little too forcefully. "I mean, no need for you to bother. You need to finish dinner, *ya*?"

Katie studied Eliza for a moment, and Eliza wondered if Katie suspected why she was so eager to tend to Gabriel's wounds. Then Katie glanced out the kitchen window, toward the barn, and said, "*Ya*. I better hurry. Levi's got his hands full." She shook her head and smiled. "Never thought I'd be *gut* at farmwork. But after I met Levi…" Katie's expression turned wistful, and she rubbed her belly, where a baby bump was just beginning to show. "Sometimes we don't know ourselves until we fall in love and see ourselves from the other's perspective."

"*Ach, Mamm*, stop being mushy," Simon piped up.

Katie and Eliza both laughed. Then Katie

pulled an alcohol wipe, a tube of antiseptic and a box of Band-Aids from the cabinet and handed them to Eliza. "Here you go. Let me know if you need anything else."

"Danki." Eliza tried not to think about what Katie had said as she hurried out the door. But the words kept turning over in her mind. How well did she actually know herself? When Gabriel said it was a challenge to figure her out, was he seeing something in her that she didn't even know was there?

Gabriel was gone when Eliza got back to his buggy. She stood there for a moment—looking one way, then another—until she realized what had happened. Eliza set the alcohol wipe, antiseptic and Band-Aids on the front seat of the buggy and headed for the barn. She felt a prick of pain in her heart when she entered through the wide double doors and into the warm, cavernous building that smelled of earth and animal. Gabriel was balanced on one leg, his crutches propped against the wall, as he used both hands to guide the bit into Comet's mouth. The horse whinnied and shook her head, sending a ripple through her brown mane.

"Gabriel, what are you doing?" Eliza asked. He needed to be taking care of himself, not trying to prove his independence. She knew that he had a reputation for slacking off, but Eliza had watched him closely enough over the years to realize he worked harder than he let on. It was almost as if he wanted people to believe he was worse than he actually was. Eliza frowned at the thought and forcefully strode over to him.

"Just doing what I always do," Gabriel said without looking away from Comet.

"Well, you don't always have a sprained ankle," Eliza said. "Not to mention all those cuts and bruises. You don't want to tear open any of your stiches, do you?"

"*Ach*, Eliza. I'm not made of glass."

Eliza sighed through her nose as she watched Gabriel struggle to keep a grip on the harness. He hopped to keep his balance, then braced his shoulder against the wall before trying again. Eliza shook her head, entered the stall, took the harness from his hands and guided the bit into Comet's mouth. Comet chomped down against the metal and snorted. Her warm breath tickled Eliza's skin, and she smiled. "See? That didn't have to be so hard, did it?"

"I almost had it," Gabriel said.

"No, you didn't."

Gabriel pushed himself away from the wall

and reached for his crutches. "You're not going to stop bossing me around, are you?"

"I'm not going to stop helping you, if that's what you're asking. You've already fallen and hurt yourself once today. That's quite enough, *ya*?"

Gabriel didn't answer. He just scowled and hobbled out of the barn, leaving Eliza to lead Comet outside.

"You know I can do that," Gabriel said when Eliza began to hitch the horse up to the buggy.

"*Ya.* And I know you can fall flat on your face too."

Gabriel gave an irritated grunt.

Eliza fastened a buckle and spun around to face him. "You know I'm right." She nodded toward his hands. "And those palms prove it."

Gabriel looked away. "I'm not as incompetent as you think," he muttered, barely loud enough for her to hear.

Eliza studied his expression for a moment. His face held a trace of pain behind the scowl. "I don't think you're incompetent, Gabriel," Eliza said in a low voice.

Gabriel's eyes shot to hers. A crinkle formed between his brows. He looked like he might say something, then shook his head and hobbled toward the buggy. "I need to get going."

"Not before I take care of those cuts."

"*Aenti* Mary has Band-Aids," Gabriel said. "I'll take care of it myself."

"You can't hold the reins unless we take care of your hands first."

"Fine. But I'll do it."

Eliza frowned. Why did he have to be so difficult? He needed help, and the practical solution was to accept it. She tried not to admit to herself that she wanted to do more than just help... She wanted to touch his hands again. She pushed the thought aside as her frown deepened. "Don't be silly. You can't do it one-handed. And you definitely can't do it with your right hand."

Gabriel looked surprised. "How did you know I'm left handed?"

Eliza clamped her mouth shut. Why had she admitted that? Now he would know that she had been watching him. For years. "I...uh... I don't know. It's just something you notice about people."

Gabriel raised an eyebrow but didn't argue. Instead, he lifted himself onto the bench seat of the buggy, set down his crutches and held out his palms. "Fine, Eliza. You win. You always do."

"What's that supposed to mean?" Eliza reached for the alcohol wipe.

"You know how you are."

Eliza's heart sank. Gabriel saw her the way everyone else did. It was *narrisch* for her to have thought otherwise. She pushed away the hurt, tore open the wipe and focused on the job at hand. "This is going to sting," she said.

"I know." But he didn't flinch when she dabbed the alcohol into his broken skin. His expression stayed as steady as a rock. *Maybe I'm not the only one who can hide pain*, Eliza thought. She wondered if Gabriel was as good at hiding emotional pain as he was at covering up physical pain. She had always suspected that he was. There was a lot more behind that handsome face and mischievous grin than he let on.

She moved on to the antiseptic, glancing up to meet his eyes to make sure she wasn't hurting him too much. Their eyes held for a moment before he looked away. "I didn't mean what I just said," he said in a quiet voice. "Or the way it sounded."

Eliza hesitated, then asked, "What *did* you mean, then?"

Gabriel let out a long breath. "That you're so…perfect."

Eliza's hand jerked to a stop. "What?" She pulled back and stared at his face. "You think I'm perfect?"

"*Ya.* Of course. You made perfect grades in school—you always knew all the answers. And you still do. You knew I needed help with Comet even though I didn't want to admit it. You knew I couldn't treat my own cuts, even though I wanted to. You also know..." His voice trailed away, and he shook his head.

Eliza could not believe what she was hearing. Her fingers tightened around his hands involuntarily. "I also know what?" she whispered.

Gabriel gave a bitter laugh. "Everything that's wrong with me."

Eliza felt the mood shift. It felt as if a dark cloud had descended, and Gabriel's features reflected the stormy air. Gabriel pulled his hands out from hers. "That's enough," he said. "I have to go."

"But..." Eliza reached for the Band-Aids.

Gabriel's jaw clenched. "I should have never let you help."

"Gabriel, you're being—"

"What? A loser? A rebel? A troublemaker?"

"No! I... Why would you say that?"

"We both know why, Eliza. We both know

what *you* think of me. What *everyone* thinks of me."

Eliza held the Band-Aid in her hand, too taken aback to move. "What *is* wrong with you, Gabriel?" she asked after a moment.

Gabriel grunted and shifted around to face the dashboard. "Everything."

Eliza shook her head, heart pounding with confusion, and set the Band-Aids beside him on the bench seat. "If you get an infection, it's your fault."

Gabriel picked up the reins and flinched. Then he set his mouth in a tight line and flicked them. Comet snorted and broke into a trot. As the buggy jerked to a start, Eliza thought she heard Gabriel whisper, "Everything always is."

Chapter Four

Eliza was reeling when she got home from work that evening. Everything that Gabriel had said echoed in her head. He had seemed so upset as he stormed away in his buggy, but she couldn't understand why. It was as though he thought she was against him—which, considering her lifelong crush on him, would be hilarious if it didn't hurt so much. She had only been trying to help.

But that was all she ever did, and somehow it always blew up in her face. In school, people used to call her Eliza the Perfect, which she didn't really understand because they meant it as an insult. Shouldn't she try to be perfect? Shouldn't everyone? She just wanted to be the best that she could be. Because if she wasn't…

Well, she didn't want to think about that. It

left her feeling panicky inside. Because if she wasn't perfect, she might not be loved.

As if on cue, the front door pushed open and her mother appeared in the doorway, hands on her hips. "Eliza, where have you been?" She narrowed her eyes. "You haven't been running off to places you shouldn't go, have you?"

"Nee, Mamm." Eliza clenched her fists by her side as she strode toward the house. "When do I ever go anywhere at all, much less someplace I shouldn't?"

Lovina ignored the comment. "You've taken care of Bunny?"

"Ya. Of course." As always, Eliza had stabled the buggy horse in their garage as soon as she returned home from work. Like other Amish who lived in town, they didn't have a barn for livestock and had to make do by converting the garage that *Englisch* builders had intended for cars.

"Priss isn't doing her homework," Lovina said. "See what you can do before supper. It's almost ready."

"Hello to you, too, *Mamm*," Eliza said quietly.

Lovina froze in the doorway. *"Ach*, I'm sorry, Eliza. What's wrong with me?" She pulled Eliza into a quick hug before she could pass through the threshold into the redbrick ranch house. "Just want to make sure everything's as it should be." Lovina pulled back and patted Eliza on the arm. "Now, let's get moving."

Eliza sighed. She had always agreed that having "everything as it should be" was important. But lately, she wasn't sure what the point was, if it made everyone feel uptight all the time. If everything were actually as it should be, wouldn't that include a sense of peace instead of stress?

"Mamm!" Priss shot into the entry hall in a blur of chubby cheeks and sparkling brown eyes. "I missed you today!"

Eliza knelt down and squeezed Priss. "I missed you too. How was your day?"

"It was *oll recht*. But Sammy Lapp splashed mud on my dress at recess. I cried a little because I didn't want it to get messed up."

Eliza pursed her lips.

"You're mad that I got my dress dirty, aren't you?" Priss asked.

Eliza realized that her expression did not match her feelings. *"Nee.* Not at all. I was just feeling bad that *you* felt bad."

"Oh." Priss held up the hem of her dress. "I tried to fix it, see?"

Priss had smeared the mud into the purple fabric, deepening the stain. Eliza almost told her not to do that again but stopped herself. "*Gut* job trying. I'm sure I can get the stain out. Don't worry." Eliza took Priss's warm, sticky hand and walked with her to the kitchen, where a notebook lay open on the table. "Now, what's this I hear about you not doing your homework?"

"*Ach*, I did do it!" Priss pointed to a row of math problems on the paper. "See?"

Eliza adjusted her glasses and studied the paper. She glanced up at Lovina, who was pulling a casserole dish from the gas oven. "*Mamm*, you said Priss wasn't doing her homework."

"Number thirteen is missing."

Eliza looked back at the homework and saw the neatly written problems numbered from one to twelve. "So she did all but the last one."

"*Ya*. She needs to do them all."

"*Ya*, but…"

Eliza could feel her mother's eyes on her, and she shifted her attention back to Lovina.

"Rebekah started slacking off in school around that age," Lovina whispered. "I should have realized that was the first sign."

"*Mamm*, Priss can hear you when you whisper, you know. She's sitting right here."

Lovina shrugged. "Well, maybe she needs to. Best she knows to mind herself so she doesn't wind up—"

"*Mamm*," Eliza said in an even but firm voice.

Lovina cut off the sentence and cleared her throat. "Supper's ready," she said and set the casserole dish onto a trivet on the counter.

"We'll figure this out after we eat," Eliza said to Priss, then kissed her on the top of her head on her way to the counter.

Eliza was even more quiet than usual during the meal. After talking about the weather, the Yoders' new milk cow and the price of corn this season, Lovina stopped, looked at Eliza and asked, "Why don't you have anything to say today?"

"I was thinking, I guess."

"About what, *Mamm*?" Priss asked.

"You remember Gabriel King?"

"Of course I do," Priss said. "He works at the Miller farm, and he always makes Simon and me laugh when I go over there to play."

Eliza smiled. "*Ya*. He likes to joke around, that's for certain sure."

Lovina's mouth tightened.

"Anyway, he's hurt his ankle and has to work in the shop for a while. He had a lot to say today."

Lovina set down her fork and shook her head. "You shouldn't be listening to that boy, Eliza. I'm sure nothing he's said is worth listening to."

"He's not so bad, *Mamm*," Eliza said quietly as she looked down at her plate. She was afraid that if she met her mother's eyes, she would give away how she felt. "Not when you get to know him." Although their time together *had* ended on a sour note that left her feeling like she had wronged him somehow.

"Humph." Lovina crossed her arms. "I don't need to get to know him. I've heard quite enough about him from others."

Priss straightened in her seat. "But Bishop Amos says that's gossip and we shouldn't listen to that." She spoke in a loud voice with an earnest, innocent expression on her face.

Lovina opened her mouth, then closed it again.

A smile twitched at the corner of Eliza's mouth. "That's right, Priss. Gossip is wrong."

Lovina shifted in her seat. Her face looked like she had just eaten an unripe persimmon. "I'm just trying to protect your *mamm*. And you."

Priss looked from Eliza to Lovina with big questioning eyes.

"We have to be careful who we spend time with and who we listen to," Lovina continued. "If we let the wrong people influence us, it can set us on the wrong path."

Eliza picked at her serving of hamburger casserole with her fork. Lovina was right about that. It *was* important not to listen to the wrong people. But something didn't sit right with her about applying that to Gabriel. She set down her fork and lifted her eyes to meet her mother's. "I don't think you know Gabriel well enough to draw these conclusions about him."

"I know he wants to leave the Amish."

Eliza shook her head hard enough to loosen a strand of hair from her *kapp*. "You don't know that for sure." Eliza would not—*could not*—believe that about Gabriel. "And besides, even if he did want to leave, wouldn't that mean we should make more effort to reach out to him?"

Lovina gave a tired sigh. She reached out and patted Eliza's hand. "I wish it were that simple. You have a *gut* heart, *dochter*, and want to help, but it just doesn't work that way."

Eliza turned her mother's words over for the rest of the meal. But no matter how much she considered Lovina's side, it just didn't feel right.

* * *

The next morning, Gabriel did not get up when his battery-powered alarm went off. He hit the snooze button and stared up at the ceiling. He couldn't go back to sleep, but he refused to face the day. One of *Aenti* Mary's roosters crowed outside his window. A door opened and closed; then he heard the rattle of dishes. The cottage was small enough to hear everything. Normally, the sound of Mary making breakfast was soothing, but today it reminded him of what he had to face. He rolled over, pulled a goose-feather pillow over his head and groaned.

After a while, Gabriel heard footsteps on the hardwood floor, then a hesitant knock. "Gabriel?" Mary's voice sounded muffled through the closed door. "Are you *oll recht*?"

"No," he grunted.

Silence.

"Go away."

"Nee."

"Ach, can't you see I need to be alone?"

"Can't you see you've got to be at work in less than an hour?"

Gabriel sighed. "I'm not going in today."

Silence. Gabriel wondered if his aunt had given up on him and walked away. Then he heard a soft, tentative reply. "*Kumme* to breakfast and we'll talk, *ya*?"

Gabriel didn't answer.

"Please?"

Gabriel pushed himself up. *Aenti* Mary had only ever been supportive of him, even if she didn't quite understand him. "*Oll recht*. Give me a minute." Gabriel could almost feel his aunt's relief through the thin walls. "*Gut,*" she said with forced cheerfulness. "And I made the *kaffi* extra strong this morning. Maybe that will help."

Kaffi wouldn't help, because waking up wasn't the problem. Facing Eliza Zook was. But how could he explain that to *Aenti* Mary? "Sounds *gut*. Thanks."

It was going to be a long day.

When Gabriel finally stumbled into the kitchen, Mary had already set the table with a heaping platter of pancakes and a plate of crispy bacon. A jar of blueberry preserves from Aunt Fannie's Gift Shop sat beside Gabriel's glass of orange juice. "Looks *gut*," Gabriel said as he settled into his chair and leaned his crutches against the wall. "*Danki.*"

Mary took a long sip of juice, then set her glass down, swallowed and folded her hands on the table in front of her. "What's wrong,

Gabriel?" She leaned forward as she waited for the answer.

Gabriel studied the crease between her brows and sighed. "Nothing," he said as he stuffed a big bite of bacon into his mouth before she could argue.

Mary raised an eyebrow and kept her eyes on him as he chewed, hands still folded in front of her. She could be so still and patient that it was unnerving. Gabriel could barely sit still long enough to finish a meal. He had too many thoughts and feelings rushing through him all the time.

Gabriel swallowed and sighed. "*Oll recht, oll recht.* Maybe there is something wrong."

Mary nodded and kept staring at him.

Gabriel flexed his jaw and speared a pancake.

"Is it your ankle?" she asked as Gabriel stared at his food. "Are you in a lot of pain?"

"*Nee.* I mean, *ya*, but that's not the problem."

"So it isn't the pain that's making you want to stay home from work today?"

"Not the kind of pain you're talking about," Gabriel said.

Mary cocked her head. "What do you mean?"

Gabriel wished he hadn't gotten out of bed—then he could have avoided his aunt's questions and wouldn't have to admit what he had done. "I mean that I feel bad. Guilty. I messed up yesterday."

"Oh." Mary's face fell. "What happened?"

"I lashed out at Eliza. She didn't deserve it. Well, she was being annoying…"

Mary gave him a look.

"…But she didn't deserve it."

Mary nodded. "Go on."

Gabriel shrugged. "What's there to say? I was my usual self. I made a mess of things. And now Eliza the Perfect knows she's right about me."

Mary clucked her tongue. "You have no right calling her that."

"Perfection is a compliment, ain't so?"

"Not when you use it as a put-down."

Gabriel grunted.

"Why are you so intimidated by her?" she asked.

He flinched and his eyes flew to Mary's. "Intimidated? I'm not…" He shook his head and laughed. "That's *narrisch*."

"No, Gabriel," Mary said in an even tone. "It's not. Why else would you always call her out like that? What has she ever done to you?"

"Plenty," Gabriel said quickly. "She's…" He tried to think of what she had actually done to him. Frowning, he shifted in his seat. "She insisted on hitching Comet up to the buggy yesterday, for starters."

"So she helped you out." Mary raised an eyebrow.

"It isn't that simple."

"Maybe it is," she said.

Gabriel shook his head. "There're plenty of other examples. She never got in trouble in school. She's never broken a single rule. Ever. In her entire life."

"I asked for examples of what she has done *to you*," Mary said.

"That *is* something…" Gabriel's voice trailed off.

"That's got nothing to do with you, and you know it."

It didn't feel that way. He thought for a moment. "She looks down on me."

"How so?" Mary leaned closer, eyes fierce with more emotion than Gabriel had seen from her in a long time. "What has she actually said or done that made you feel that way?"

"Uh, well… She…" Gabriel scowled. "I can't remember any specific examples, but—"

"That's because there aren't any, Gabriel King."

"You don't know that. She's always making me feel like a loser compared to her. And she's always bossing me around like she knows best."

"The fact that she follows the rules and tries her best has got nothing to do with you. If that makes you feel bad, then you probably need to work on yourself instead of pointing fingers."

"Ouch! Whose side are you on, anyway, *Aenti* Mary?" Gabriel set down his fork with a clang.

"There aren't sides to this. Just facts."

"And the fact is, I'm the loser."

"That is *not* what I said."

"But it's what you meant."

Mary threw up her hands. "Why do you have to be so impossible? Can't you see how *gut* you are? Can't you see how much I love you? How much everybody who knows you loves you?"

Gabriel swallowed hard and kept his eyes on his plate. "Not everyone."

The room filled with uncomfortable silence.

"Your *daed* is wrong about you," Mary said after a moment. "And he does love you. In his own way."

"He has a funny way of showing it."

His aunt sighed. "There is no excuse for how hard he has been on you, and I won't try to make any for him."

Gabriel nodded. He appreciated that.

"But Eliza has nothing to do with any of that."

Gabriel felt a pang of guilt. Of course Mary was right. He knew that he had been unfair to Eliza ever since he stormed away from the Miller farm yesterday. He sighed and pushed his plate away without eating any of his pancakes. "I guess I better get to work." It was the last place he wanted to go, and Eliza was the last person he wanted to see. But he knew he had to make things right.

Eliza's *mamm* usually watched Priss after school and on Saturdays while Eliza worked at the gift shop. But Lovina was going to a quilting bee in a neighboring church district on Saturday to visit with old friends. Eliza had arranged for the Millers' next-door neighbor, Sadie Lapp, to watch Priss that morning. But when Eliza arrived at Sadie's door, the young woman cracked it open and sneezed into a tissue. "I'm sorry," she said in a hoarse voice. "We're all down with a bad cold. I don't think Priss should *kumme* in, or she'll catch it." Sadie's blue eyes didn't have their usual sparkle, and her blonde hair looked disheveled beneath her *kapp*.

"*Ach*, Sadie, you look terrible."

Sadie looked taken aback for a moment, then shook her head and laughed. "You never mince words, do you, Eliza?"

Eliza pushed her glasses up her nose. "Did I say the wrong thing? You only look terrible because you normally look so pretty."

Sadie laughed again. "You're honest, anyway."

Eliza sighed and looked down. She had not meant to be rude. "I'm sorry. I didn't mean—"

"It's *oll recht*," Sadie interrupted. "I know what you meant. You've got a *gut* heart, Eliza, even though not everyone understands that."

Eliza's gaze shot back up to Sadie. "Now who's being too honest?" she asked with a wry smile.

Sadie returned the smile. "You're right. I didn't have to add that last point."

Eliza shrugged. "Well, it is true, so I can't fault you." Most people didn't understand her, that was certain sure.

Sadie shook her head. "Still, I probably shouldn't have said it."

They stared at each other awkwardly for a few beats. Eliza wanted to tell Sadie how much she liked her and that she appreciated her honesty, but she wasn't sure how to put that into words. "Well, I better get going," Eliza said after a moment. "I hope you feel better soon."

"I'm sorry I can't watch Priss today. Maybe Katie can give you the day off or let you leave early."

"The Millers are going to be gone all day. They're at a livestock auction. But don't worry—we'll manage." Eliza looked down at Priss and squeezed her hand. "Won't we?"

Priss nodded as she looked up at Eliza with her big brown eyes.

Eliza switched her attention back to Sadie. "You just focus on getting better. Don't wear yourself out taking care of everyone." Sadie had six younger siblings, and she stayed busy helping her mother care for them.

"Thanks, Eliza." Sadie paused to cough into her tissue. "I'll try not to."

"Oh, and don't worry if you're a little late filling that order. We can manage." Sadie was a talented artist who sold her art at the gift shop.

"*Nee*, I'll get it all to you on time."

Eliza nodded. Sadie was serious about her work and always kept her commitments. Eliza appreciated that about her. As she and Priss cut across the yard to the Millers' property, Eliza turned that thought over in her mind. Gabriel was known for *not* keeping his commitments.

So why was she so taken by him? Perhaps her *mamm* was right. Eliza might be so blinded by love that she wasn't willing to see the truth. The thought made her stomach feel heavy, as if she had swallowed a stone.

Worse, what would Lovina say if she found out that Priss was spending the day with Gabriel King? Lovina would think that his rebellious ways would rub off on Priss for certain sure, even though Eliza would be there to supervise. Instead of trusting her, Lovina would probably blame Eliza for exposing Priss to a 'bad influence,' even though there was nothing she could do about it—and nothing that dangerous about Gabriel, anyway.

That stone in the pit of her stomach continued to weigh her down as she and Priss unlocked the door to the shop, strode inside and opened the shutters. Crisp yellow sunlight streamed across the worn hardwood floors and shone against a row of glass jars filled with raspberry preserves. Gabriel wasn't there yet. She glanced at the clock on the wall. He was late. Another sign that Lovina was right—at least a little bit.

"I wish Simon was here," Priss said. "Today is going to be real boring without him."

Eliza gazed distractedly out the window,

looking for Gabriel's buggy to appear on the road. Priss tugged on her *mamm's* apron. "What's there for me to do here?"

Eliza pulled her attention from the road. "*Ach,* I don't know… But I'm sure we'll find something. Maybe you can help me dust?"

Priss pushed out her bottom lip. "That doesn't sound very fun."

Eliza sighed. "It's *gut* to work. Life isn't always about having fun."

"But I was supposed to play with the Lapps today." Several of Sadie's younger siblings were around Priss's age.

Eliza looked around the shop, wondering what Priss could do to keep busy. She could ask her to straighten some of the displays, but she might do more harm than *gut*, and Eliza couldn't risk that. A lot of the goods in the gift shop were delicate and breakable.

The familiar clip-clop of hooves against pavement interrupted Eliza's thoughts. She peered out the window to see Gabriel's buggy trudging down the road. She checked the time. Fifteen minutes late. Not terrible—but not okay either.

The shop felt too quiet as Eliza waited for Gabriel to unhitch Comet and put her in the south pasture. The only sound was an occasional sigh from Priss as she sat slumped near the window, staring at the clouds drifting across the bright blue sky.

"Can I go outside and play?" Priss asked.

"No. You could get hurt. Remember that time we thought Simon had fallen into the grain bin?"

"But he didn't. You just *thought* he had."

Eliza swept her gaze across the muddy farmyard, which was overshadowed by the squat, round grain bin and tall, narrow silo. A few chickens pecked at the earth beside a rusted, broken tractor. The cows grazed in a field behind the red barn, and a row of black stockings and white shirts flapped on the clothesline beside the rambling white farmhouse. Nearby, the metal blades of the windmill whined as they turned in the wind above the pond. "You might fall into the pond."

"I won't go near it."

"There's a lot of mud from all the snowmelt and spring rain."

"Not on the porch." The farmhouse had a spacious wraparound porch lined with white rocking chairs.

Eliza considered this for a moment, then shook her head. "*Nee*, it's best to keep you inside."

Priss sighed and kept staring at the sky.

The door to the shop swung open as the bell rang out cheerfully.

"Hello!" Gabriel said to Priss. "What's this? A new shopkeeper to help us today?"

Priss turned from the window, and her posture straightened. *"Ya."* She nodded, grinned and glanced at Eliza. "I'm a real shopkeeper now, just like you. Ain't so, *Mamm*?"

Eliza smiled. "For certain sure." Then she raised an eyebrow. "But you have to dust to be considered a real shopkeeper."

"Ach, okay… I guess I can do that."

Gabriel grinned. "I'll help."

"But you can't. You're on crutches."

"I didn't say I'd help dust. I'll help make it fun."

Priss looked intrigued. *"Oll recht."*

"First thing, we need dusters." Gabriel looked to Eliza as he hobbled toward his chair behind the counter. "Good morning, by the way. Sorry I'm late."

Eliza was too impressed by his interaction with Priss to scold him. "That's okay. Just don't make a habit of it."

Gabriel gave an exaggerated look of surprise. "What? No criticism?"

Eliza rolled her eyes, marched to a cabinet

behind the counter, pulled out two feather dusters and slapped them onto the counter.

Gabriel chuckled, took off his straw hat and replaced it with one of the feather dusters. "What do you think, Priss?"

Priss laughed. "That's not right!"

"*Nee?* I thought it made a *gut* hat."

Eliza couldn't help but chuckle at the sight of Gabriel with a wad of feathers covering his hair.

"I guess you'll have to show me how to use it, then."

"Like this!" Priss said as she grabbed the other duster. She skipped to the nearest shelf and began to run the feathers over a stack of crocheted doilies.

"Ah! I had no idea," Gabriel said. "I still like it as a hat."

Eliza shook her head and laughed.

Gabriel turned to her. "I think I just heard Eliza Zook giggle. Never thought I'd see the day."

"That was not a giggle, Gabriel. It was a chuckle. A very subdued chuckle."

"Po-tay-to, po-tah-to," Gabriel responded with a wink.

Eliza shook her head. "You are impossible."

"Then why are you still smiling?"

Eliza's eyes looked at his, and she tried to frown but couldn't manage it. She felt herself falling into his gleaming green eyes and experiencing the lighthearted way he saw the world along with him. She loved him for that. He brought such a wonderful energy to her dull, predictable life.

Eliza caught herself. She was supposed to be upset with Gabriel after the way he'd stormed off yesterday. Or at least cautious. She should not indulge in silly, lovestruck emotions. "I better go over inventory," she said curtly and hurried away.

Eliza tried to focus on the ledger in front of her, but Gabriel's antics distracted her. Every time Priss grew bored, he thought of something new to entertain her. At the moment, he was singing a silly song that described everything she did as she dusted. Eliza couldn't help but be impressed by Gabriel's wit. He seemed to have the ability to rhyme any word in an instant.

When he finally ran out of steam, Gabriel slapped a hand on the counter and announced it was time for a snack.

"Ya!" Priss echoed. "Time for a snack!"

Eliza closed the ledger and stood up. "I'll be right back." The gift shop didn't have a kitchen, but the Millers always left their door unlocked, and she had free rein to use theirs as needed. "I have a strawberry Jell-O salad in the Millers' refrigerator."

Gabriel waved Eliza toward him. She walked closer and he motioned for her to lower her head. "Why don't you send Priss?" he whispered quietly enough not to be overheard.

Eliza frowned and shook her head. "The farmyard isn't safe…"

"The most dangerous thing out there is a couple of hens."

"There's farm equipment, livestock—"

"Not between here and the house. It's a thirty-second walk." He hesitated, then added, "Besides, I want to talk to you. Alone."

Her heart did a little flip-flop in her chest. Gabriel wanted to talk to her alone! Eliza straightened up. Gabriel watched her with raised eyebrows. After a moment, Eliza shook her head and sighed. "*Oll recht.* I'll let her go."

Gabriel nodded. *"Gut."*

Eliza gave Priss clear, simple instructions and sent her on her way. The little girl skipped out the door with a huge grin on her face. "I can do lots of things all by myself," she said before trotting down the front steps and into the yard.

Eliza sat down on a stool beside Gabriel and pushed her glasses up the bridge of her nose. Her heart pounded so hard she was afraid he might see the movement through her dress. "You wanted to talk to me?"

Gabriel inhaled, held it for a moment and then released a big puff of air. "Uh, *ya*. I, um…" He cleared his throat and shifted in his seat. "I owe you an apology."

Eliza stared at him.

"For yesterday."

Eliza nodded.

"I shouldn't have criticized you for trying to help me. I shouldn't have accused you of thinking the worst of me…" Gabriel frowned and looked down at the counter. "You won't understand this, but you make me feel bad about myself."

Eliza winced.

Gabriel responded with a quick, bitter laugh. "You've never been in trouble in your life. You've probably never even broken a single rule. Ever."

"But what does that have to do with you?"

"You're so perfect that it highlights how imperfect I am."

"I am far from perfect, Gabriel."

Gabriel shrugged. "You sure seem like it."

"I come across as prideful, you mean?"

Gabriel furrowed his brow and thought for a moment. "Not exactly. You come across as always knowing that you're right."

"Is that such a bad thing?"

Gabriel grunted. "Maybe not. If you really *are* right, that is."

"Gabriel, I don't think that *I'm* right. I think that our ways are right. I think the *Ordnung* is right. I think—no, I *know*—*Gott* is right." She held up her hands. "I just want to keep His ways."

Gabriel leaned closer to her. "Ya, *Gott* is always right. But how do you know *Gott*'s ways are the same as our ways?"

Eliza inhaled sharply.

Gabriel stared into her eyes.

"Because… Because…" Eliza pulled her gaze from his and stood up. She shook her head. "You shouldn't ask these questions."

"I think I should," Gabriel said in the most serious voice Eliza had ever heard him use. "And I think you should too."

Chapter Five

Lovina was right. Gabriel was dangerous. He was encouraging her to question the *Ordnung*. Without that framework, what did she have? What did any of them have? You had to have rules to keep order and know what to do. Without rules, the world would fall apart around them all.

Thoughts and questions nibbled at Eliza for the rest of the day. She barely noticed Priss's enthusiasm on the ride home or how she volunteered to help cook supper that night. "Gabriel says I'm *gut* at lots of stuff, ain't so? Bet I'm *gut* at cooking too."

Eliza was taken aback at how suddenly he had developed such an influence over the child. No—over *both* of them. Eliza did not want to admit it, but he had already planted rebellious thoughts in her own mind. What if he did the same to Priss, just like Lovina had warned?

Eliza barely slept that night. She climbed out of bed to pace after the moon had slipped below the horizon and the only light came from the faint glow of streetlights along Bluebird Hill's Main Street a quarter mile away. The world felt too silent as she wrestled with her emotions. Not even a dog barked. Not a single car or truck zipped passed the redbrick ranch house on their way downtown. She was alone.

Or was she? Eliza padded across the braided-rag rug in her bare feet, then shook her head, lowered herself to her knees beside her bed, propped her elbows on the mattress and folded her hands. "I don't know what to say, *Gott*." She paused, unfolded and refolded her hands. "Show me clearly how Gabriel is wrong. And show him too. Amen."

Eliza started to rise, then heaved a heavy sigh and squeezed her eyes shut. "*Oll recht*, maybe that wasn't quite right, *Gott*. Please show Gabriel and me *if* he's wrong." She shifted her weight. "And show me if I'm wrong about…anything. I know you have rules that you want me to keep. Just please make sure I'm keeping the right ones. *Danki*. Amen."

Eliza rose and slipped back under the warm, colorful quilt. She fell asleep almost immediately.

Gabriel had tried to apologize and failed. He couldn't even manage to do that right. Instead, he had made a wild suggestion to Eliza that she clearly was not ready to hear.

Maybe he was wrong to even think it himself.

He never should have planted doubt in Eliza's mind. Her steadfastness and confidence was one of the things he admired most about her.

Gabriel stopped himself. *Admired?* He admired Eliza Zook? He shook his head and chuckled. Well, he supposed he did. After spending a few days with her in the shop, he had gotten to know her for the first time, even though he had been around her for years. Suddenly, she was no longer a flat character but a three-dimensional person. There was so much more to her than met the eye.

He even admired her no-nonsense way of dealing with life, even if it was a bit frustrating at times. In fact, that little frown she got when she was acting so serious was kind of cute. Gabriel shook his head again. Maybe he *had* gotten a head injury in that accident with Thunder, because these thoughts were *narrisch*.

"Are you *oll recht*?" *Aenti* Mary turned to look at him from where she sat beside him in the buggy on the way to Viola Esch's house, where church was being held today.

"What?" Gabriel adjusted the reins in his hands. "*Ya*. Why wouldn't I be?"

"You're quiet," Mary said. "Too quiet." She squinted suspiciously at him. "Usually means you're up to no *gut*."

"I wish."

Mary cocked her head. "You wish?"

Gabriel chuckled. "Never mind. I just meant that would be easier than…"

"Easier than what?"

Easier than having strange thoughts about Eliza Zook. "*Ach*, it's nothing." He nodded toward a beige farmhouse with potted plants lining the front porch and a row of gray buggies parked in the yard. "Anyway, we're here."

"Lucky for you," Mary said.

"*Ya*." Gabriel grinned.

"But don't think I'm going to forget about how strange you're acting. I know something's on your mind."

"And you'll bring it back up later, I'm sure."

Mary laughed and patted his arm. "What's an *aenti* for?"

"Baking pies?" Gabriel asked with exaggerated innocence.

She gave him a playful punch in the biceps. "That's enough out of you, young man."

"You know you're young enough to be my sister, right? No matter how old you like to act."

Mary raised her chin and smiled. "But I'm not your sister, even though I'm only thirty-three. I'm your *aenti*, so you have to listen to me."

"If you say so," Gabriel said with a wry grin.

"I do." She waited a few beats, then added, "Don't worry about whatever it is that's troubling you. Give it to *Gott*. He'll work it out for the best."

Gabriel thought about what he had told Eliza and all the questions that had been turning around in his own mind lately. "What if..." Gabriel pulled on the reins to slow Comet as they neared Viola's driveway.

"Ya?"

"What if I'm in the wrong?"

"Then trust Him to tell you."

"You make it sound so simple."

"Well, you have to be willing to listen—and

to admit you're wrong, if that's what He lays on your heart."

Gott and the *Ordnung* were so tangled up together that he didn't know how to separate them, much less talk to *Gott* about it. Gabriel was glad to shove the thought aside when they reached the turnoff. He guided Comet toward the big enclosed wagon that carried the church benches from house to house and the line of buggies already parked in the grass. The wheels sank into the soft earth as they bumped along. They hit a pothole and Mary bounced up from the bench seat, slammed back down onto the seat and laughed. "That one got me," she said.

Gabriel flinched. "I'm sorry. I should have been more careful."

"Nonsense," Mary said. "It's not your fault that the ground is uneven here. Besides, it gave me a *gut* laugh. Sometimes life gets too predictable, and you can use a little shake-up. Pun intended."

Gabriel thought about that for a moment. He wondered what Eliza would say about shaking things up in life. "Whoa, girl," he said and tugged on the reins. Comet snorted, tossed her head and slowed to a stop. The buggy rocked back, then lay still, and Gabriel pulled the hand brake. He glanced over to see Mary looking at him. "What?"

"A lot of things that you think are your fault, aren't. I hope you know that."

Gabriel tried to dismiss her comment with a playful grin. "What's made you so serious all the sudden?"

Mary shook her head but kept her eyes on him. "Since you apologized for no reason. You do that a lot, you know. You're always taking blame when there's none to take." She put a hand on his forearm. "I should tell you this more often. You need to hear it."

"*Ach,* I don't know." Gabriel didn't know how to handle the emotions that Mary's statement brought up inside him. He would rather push them away and think of something else. "We better get inside." Gabriel nodded toward the plastic container on the back seat. "Don't forget the whoopie pies." Then he hopped out of the buggy and onto his good foot, grabbed his crutches, and hobbled away before his aunt could say another word.

As soon as Gabriel stepped into the house, he was immediately surrounded by a flock of concerned women, most of whom were young and single. "Gabriel!" Sarah Yoder said as she rested her hand on his elbow. "We heard you were almost killed wrangling a runaway horse."

"You poor thing!" Rachel Peachy exclaimed, nudging Sarah aside.

"Let me help you," Lydia Kauffman said as she pushed her way to his side.

"Now, now," a stern, elderly voice announced from the back of the group. "Let the boy breathe." Viola Esch shuffled toward Gabriel, using her cane to part the crowd. Viola's stark-white hair and bent posture showed her ninety-two years, but the decades had not dimmed her indomitable spirit—or her belief that she knew best. "Stop clucking like a bunch of hens, and show some dignity." When she reached Gabriel's side, she pointed her cane at Rachel, then Sarah. "When I was your age, *maedels* didn't throw themselves at *buwe*" She shook her head. "It just wasn't done."

"*Ach*, Viola, they're just asking if I'm *oll recht*," Gabriel said with a sheepish expression.

"Humph." Viola looked down her nose at the young women. "Go on, now." She made a shooing motion with her hand. "You should be helping your mothers mind the children, ain't so? The service is about to start." Sarah, Rachel and Lydia glanced at one another, then hurried away. Viola watched them leave with her hands on her hips. Then she nodded and looked up at Gabriel. "You're welcome."

Gabriel sighed. "Not sure I want to thank you for that. They were just being nice."

"Nonsense. Those girls shouldn't throw themselves at you like that. It isn't proper."

Gabriel knew better than to argue with Viola. It would be pointless. He had always appreciated attention from girls—and they usually seemed eager to give him that attention—but he had never felt serious about any girl before. He just liked knowing that they thought he was *gut* enough. Of course, since he never got close to any of them they only liked him for his looks and his bravado. That had always been enough, though.

Until now. Gabriel couldn't understand it, but something about his interaction with Sarah, Rachel and Lydia this morning had felt…empty. Another sign of a head injury.

"What's the matter with you?" Viola's voice broke into Gabriel's thoughts. "Can't you see Bishop Amos is almost ready to start the service?"

"What?" Gabriel's attention jerked back to his surroundings.

"Go sit down." Viola motioned toward the men's section. The able-bodied men had already moved Viola's glider, sofa, quilt rack and propane lampstand from her living room and replaced the furniture with long, backless benches.

Gabriel couldn't help but notice Eliza sitting on one of the benches in the women's section as he hobbled to take his place on the men's side of the room. Her posture was straight and proper, her hands clasped neatly in her lap. Priss and Lovina flanked her, both sitting silently, eyes on Bishop Amos, who stood between the two sections. Priss began to swing her legs. Eliza shook her head slightly and gently patted Priss's knee. The little girl stopped and sat as still as her aunt and grandmother.

Gabriel realized that he wanted Eliza to look over at him, which was ridiculous. A handful of pretty, popular girls had lined up to fawn over him that morning. Any young, single man in the church district would be thrilled by that. But for some strange reason, he would rather have had Eliza pay him attention.

She wasn't popular, and he'd never considered her pretty before. People just didn't think of her that way. But as he studied her face from across the room, he noticed that her thin, straight nose was perfectly suited to her face. And her high, sharp cheekbones gave her a regal look. In fact, she was…pretty. Very pretty. How had he never noticed before? How had no one noticed before?

Maybe it was because her beauty came from within and became clearer the more you got to know her. He suspected that most people—and most men, in particular—had never made the effort to get to know her.

He stared at Eliza for another moment, but she never looked his way. She never gave any sign that she felt his eyes on her at all. Her attention stayed steadfastly on Bishop Amos. Gabriel finally turned his gaze to the front of the room when Bishop Amos raised his hands to quiet the murmuring and begin the service. But he kept thinking about the fact that Eliza Zook was the only young, single woman in the room who was ignoring him.

And she was the only woman in the room he had any interest in getting to know better.

Eliza could not believe what she had seen that morning. All the girls in the church district were throwing themselves at Gabriel like he was a big handsome hero. Well, he *was* handsome. But all he had done was get himself dragged behind a horse. She was the one who had stopped it. But no one acknowledged that. They all wanted to fawn over Gabriel and flirt with him. It irked her so much that she refused to look at him.

Maybe what truly irked her was the fact that all the other young women were pretty and popular and that Gabriel obviously loved the attention. But she didn't want to admit that to herself. It wasn't as if she were in competition with those girls. That would be impossible. Best to stop thinking about Gabriel King, keep her eyes on the preacher and forget the feelings she had for him. Because there was no way he would ever return those feelings for her when he had all those other girls to choose from. That was certain sure. In fact, he probably wouldn't like her in that way if she were the last woman on earth. Why would he want to court an old stick-in-the-mud with big glasses who always said the wrong thing?

After the three-hour service wound to a close, Eliza hurried out of her seat to help with lunch. They had all brought food and quickly laid out plates of thick-sliced homemade bread with Amish peanut butter spread, jellied salads, slices of cold ham, pickled beets, pretzels, cheese cubes, schnitz pies, whoopie pies and plenty of black coffee and iced tea.

As with any Amish gathering, the men would

eat first, and Eliza fell back to a corner of the kitchen as the men worked their way down the buffet line. Priss hopped from one foot to the other as she waited.

"Stay still, please," Lovina said to Priss as she reached into one of Viola's kitchen drawers for a serving fork, then zipped away to place it beside the platter of ham. Priss sighed and stood still. She looked up at Eliza and tugged the sleeve of her blue cape dress. "Can I go outside and play with Simon and the other *kinner* until it's our turn to eat?"

Eliza glanced through the kitchen window above the sink. Simon was crouched in the backyard, petting one of Viola's dogs. He grinned as he ruffled the dog's fur, looked up, noticed her and waved. Eliza waved back and looked away.

"Can I?" Priss asked, tugging harder on Eliza's sleeve. Eliza hesitated. She didn't know what trouble Priss might get into. And what if Viola's dog was a biter? Or what if she came back inside with a muddy dress? How would that look? Eliza always worried that people thought she wasn't a good-enough mother. Children shouldn't be running around in the dirt on a church Sunday.

But then Eliza noticed Gabriel in the serving

line. Yesterday, he had been so casually reassuring about Priss going outside on her own. He didn't think she would get hurt. And he wouldn't judge either of them if Priss got her dress dirty or lost her *kapp*. Eliza remembered how happy Priss had been to walk to the Millers' kitchen all by herself. She had been filled with a confidence that Eliza rarely saw in her. *"Oll recht,"* Eliza blurted out before she could change her mind. "Go on."

Priss darted toward the door. *"Danki, Mamm!"*

"But don't get dirty. And stay out of trouble."

Priss was gone so fast that Eliza doubted she had heard her.

Eliza's eyes moved back to Gabriel as he hobbled down the buffet line. Sarah and Lydia flanked his side, each holding a plate for him as he pointed out what he wanted to eat. Of course he couldn't hold his own plate while he gripped his crutches, but Eliza felt a pang of indignation nonetheless. She couldn't bear to see those two weasel their way into his heart with plates of whoopie pies and pickled beets.

Eliza rubbed her temples. She wasn't being fair. It was only right that Lydia and Sarah should help out. It wasn't their fault that they were prettier and more popular than she was.

But it still stung.

Gabriel looked up, and Eliza jerked her eyes away before he could see her staring. She ought to accept that he would choose Lydia or Sarah, or some other girl just like them.

When it was time for the women to eat, Eliza could barely taste her food and excused herself without finishing her schnitz pie. She hid in the kitchen, stealing a few sips of black *kaffi* before clearing the buffet table and wiping the counters. The *kaffi* grew cold while she worked, and she poured the last half of it down the sink. *This is why* Englischers *have microwaves*, she thought. What would life be like if you could just press a button and reheat a drink in fifteen seconds? Was that what drew Gabriel toward the *Englisch*? Did he think it would be easier, more convenient? She supposed it would be. But it would also be lonely and purposeless without the community that anchored them.

She listened to the low murmur of voices from the other side of the wall, where the long benches had been converted to tables. A child laughed. One of Viola's dogs barked. A few moments later, Viola rushed past the kitchen, shooing the animal toward the back door. "Who let you in?" she muttered as she used her cane to hobble at double speed behind the dog. Eliza smiled as she heard the screen door squeak open, followed by a happy yip. An instant later, she saw the dog tear across the yard, then disappear beyond the view of the kitchen window.

Bluebird Hills wasn't perfect, but it was perfect for her. Even if Gabriel's comments did make her question things she had never questioned before. She adjusted her *kapp* and smoothed her apron. She liked knowing what to wear, what to expect. She liked the feeling of safety and continuity that the *Ordnung* brought. Why couldn't Gabriel see that? Why couldn't he feel the same way? She didn't know if you *had* to have the *Ordnung* to have *Gott*, but she knew it made her feel closer to Him. And she didn't want to give up that closeness. Not for anything in the world.

"You didn't eat."

Eliza spun around from the window to see Viola leaning against the kitchen doorway.

"*Ach*, I had enough." Leave it to Viola to notice that Eliza had left most of her food untouched. The old woman seemed to know everything about everyone in the entire church district.

"Why are you hiding out in the kitchen? Avoiding someone?" Viola asked.

Eliza flinched before she managed to hide her surprise.

Viola thumped her cane on the linoleum floor. "I thought so."

"*Nee*, I just wanted to get a start on the cleanup."

"Eliza Zook, I wasn't born yesterday."

"*Nee*. I suppose not."

Viola shuffled closer to Eliza. "Couldn't help but notice Gabriel King has been getting a lot of attention today."

"Has he? I didn't notice." Eliza popped a lid onto a plastic container that held a few leftover whoopie pies.

Viola tapped her cane against the floor again. "That's enough. I've seen you around Gabriel. I know how you feel about him."

Eliza's hands fumbled against the plastic container and she dropped it, her stomach lurching to the floor along with it. "How could you…?" She crouched to pick up the whoopie pies. "*Nee*, you couldn't… That's not…"

"I already told you, I wasn't born yesterday. I imagine you've gotten closer to Gabriel since he's been working in the shop. From what I can tell, he's barely spoken to you before." Viola glanced backward, over her shoulder, then returned her attention to Eliza. "Now, Lovina won't like me saying this, but I'll say it straight to her face if need be. Gabriel King has *gut* in him. I'm sure of it."

Eliza swallowed hard and straightened back up. Her hands trembled as she gripped the plastic container of pies. "*Ya.* I know."

Viola nodded. "Of course you do. Otherwise you wouldn't have fallen for him. Problem is, most people don't see it."

Eliza nodded.

"What he needs is someone who understands our ways and our rules. Someone who can show him the *gut* in it."

Eliza felt as if she had been struck. "You mean…"

"Show him, Eliza. As Amish, we know that everything that happens to us is *Gott's* will. So that business with the horse, his having to work with you at the shop—it's all part of *Gott's* plan. So you better take this opportunity to help him find his way, Eliza. You might not get another chance."

And with that, Viola wheeled around and shuffled out of the room. Eliza was too dumbstruck to react. She just stood there, staring at the doorway, clutching the plastic container while her mind filled with new possibilities.

If Viola was right, then maybe she should

try harder to win Gabriel's affection instead of just pining after him from afar. Maybe it was the responsible thing to do to go after him. She picked up the damp dishrag and began wiping the counter when an idea slipped into her head. Her hand froze. The idea was a little *narrisch*, but she was willing to do something outlandish for Gabriel, especially if could help him find his way.

She slowly ran the dishrag across the counter as the plan set in her mind.

But could she really go through with it?

Chapter Six

Gabriel whistled as he entered the gift shop on Monday morning. He felt inexplicably light-hearted about spending the day with Eliza. Whatever she did or said was sure to be interesting and would probably challenge his way of thinking. She seemed to have that effect on him.

"Hello? Can I help you?" Eliza called out.

Gabriel saw her standing at the end of the aisle, staring at him. It took him a few beats to register what was different about her, then realized she wasn't wearing her big, round glasses. "It's me."

"*Ach*, of course. I knew that." She gave her signature frown for an instant; then her face snapped into a syrupy sweet smile. The expression did not fit her at all. "*Kumme*, sit and prop up that poor ankle of yours. I've got a cold glass of lemonade waiting for you."

Gabriel gave her a suspicious look. Something wasn't right here. Eliza was never this considerate. She was usually too busy telling him why he was wrong about something. "Um. *Oll recht.*" He studied her with narrowed eyes.

Eliza rushed to his side as soon as he settled into his chair and shoved the glass of lemonade in his hand. He took a slow sip as he looked up at her. She hovered above him, hands clasped in front of her. The lemonade did hit the spot. "Mmm, *danki.* That's real *gut.*"

"It's fresh squeezed. I made it this morning." She hesitated and swallowed hard. "Just for you."

Gabriel shifted in his seat. What was going on? Eliza was being way too nice. "Uh, okay."

Eliza stared at him for a few beats. "I could get you something else…"

Gabriel shook his head. "*Nee.* I'm fine."

"Um, what about something to eat? I brought peanut butter cookies. I made them last night." She hesitated again. "For you."

Gabriel cleared his throat. This was getting awkward. "*Nee,* I just ate breakfast. Besides, it's a little early in the day for sweets, ain't so?"

Eliza's face fell. "*Ya*, of course it is." Her finger flew to the bridge of her nose to push up her glasses, which weren't there.

"Old habits die hard, huh?" Gabriel asked.

"What?"

"Your glasses. You were going to push them into place, but they're not there."

"Oh. *Ya*."

"Why aren't you wearing them, anyway?"

"*Ach*, no reason." Eliza turned away abruptly, grabbed an embroidered cushion from a shelf beneath the counter and held it up. "I brought this for you from home." She bent over his ankle, gently lifted his leg from where it was propped on the crate and placed the cushion beneath his foot. "Better?" She carefully lowered his ankle and released his leg.

Gabriel grinned. "*Ya*. Much better. *Danki*."

Eliza nodded. "*Gut*." She hovered over him for a moment. "Well, I better get to work." She disappeared behind a row of shelves, and Gabriel sat quietly, drumming his fingers and taking slow sips of lemonade. Every so often, he heard a bang or a crash, followed by a surprised yelp. "Did you break your glasses?" he called across the store. "Or just lose them?"

"Sorry, can't hear you!" Eliza called out, right before another thump. Several balls of yarn rolled out from behind the shelf and into Gabriel's view.

The bell above the door rang, and Sadie Lapp walked into the shop, a wooden crate propped on her hip.

"How can I help you?" Eliza asked.

"Eliza, it's me, Sadie. Don't you recognize me?" She laughed and kept walking toward the counter. "I brought some paintings." She dropped the crate onto the counter with a thud, stretched her arms and grinned. Her blue eyes sparkled. "I think Katie will like these." She glanced around. "Where is she? We had planned to meet today." Even though Katie stopped working behind the counter when she married Levi, she still made most of the decisions involving the business.

"She had to help Simon take his amphibian collection to school today. He's giving a presentation on local wildlife."

Sadie smiled. "Sounds like Simon."

"I guess I can take a look at your paintings for her since she's running late." Eliza said.

Sadie's smile faded. "I can wait for Katie."

"*Nee*, I'll take care of it."

Eliza marched around the corner of the display shelves and made a beeline for the crate. She glanced inside but didn't flip through any of the canvases. "Looks *gut*. We'll take them all."

Sadie looked surprised. "You will?"

"I'm sure Katie would take them all."

"*Ya*, but…you're not Katie."

Eliza sniffed and gave Sadie an indignant look. "I appreciate art, too, you know."

Sadie raised an eyebrow.

"*Oll recht*, I'll take a closer look." She pulled out the first canvas, squinted at it and moved it closer to her eyes. "Looks…creative."

"And that's a *gut* thing or a bad thing?" Sadie asked.

"*Gut.*"

Sadie slid her hands to her hips. "Eliza Zook, what has gotten into you?"

Eliza pursed her lips.

"Maybe I can finally be of some use around here," Gabriel said. "Let's see what you've got, Sadie." He leaned across the counter and scooted the crate toward him, then pulled out the first canvas and studied it. The painting depicted a bleak winter landscape in different hues of blue. "The snow's blue," he said.

Eliza's face twitched into what almost looked like a smile.

"*Ya*," Sadie said without elaborating.

Gabriel didn't understand, but he didn't want

to hurt Sadie's feelings, so he set the painting aside and picked up the next one. He thought he saw a pond that reflected a forest, but he couldn't quite tell. The images were blurry and only suggested the outlines of trees…if they *were* trees. Could be a fuzzy field of corn. He cleared his throat. "Um, this is…interesting."

"Danki," Sadie said. There was an awkward silence.

The door opened and Katie Miller swept inside. *"Gude Mariye,* she said to Eliza and Gabriel before turning to Sadie. "Sorry I'm running late to meet you this morning."

Sadie looked relieved. "That's *oll recht. I know you're busy. But I hope you still have time to take a look?"*

Katie grinned. *"Ya,* I can't wait. Your paintings have helped put our little shop on the map, you know. Tourists *kumme* looking for this place now."

Eliza nodded, but her expression looked dubious.

Katie looked down at the painting of blue snow and clapped her hands. "I love this one! So moving. It captures the wistful beauty of winter." She glanced over to Gabriel. "Ain't so?"

Gabriel frowned and cleared his throat.

"Um, *ya*… I guess." He squinted at the painting, but all he saw was a lot of shades of blue. He didn't feel wistful at all. Something must be wrong with him, because everyone else seemed to get it—even Eliza, which didn't make sense. If he could count on anyone to maintain a no-nonsense approach to art, it should be Eliza.

"It's very *gut*," Eliza said in a matter-of-fact tone.

Katie's attention shot to Eliza. "You finally agree with me about Sadie's art?"

Eliza shifted her weight from one foot to the other. "It's not that I didn't always agree…" She glanced at Gabriel, then back to the painting. "I've always liked…um…the color blue." She raised her chin a fraction before declaring, "You know, I'm not as uptight and serious as people think. I do have an imagination."

Sadie stifled a laugh behind her hand. Katie raised her eyebrows but didn't argue. Instead, she turned her attention to Sadie. "We'll take all of them. Same commission rate as always."

Sadie beamed as she unloaded the rest of the canvases from the crate. *"Danki."*

"So, Gabriel," Katie said as soon as Sadie had left with her empty crate, "how do you like working in the shop?"

He thought about the question for a moment. At first, he would have said he didn't like it at all. But now, after a few days spent with Eliza, he was actually starting to enjoy his time here. Even if she had been acting a little strange today. "I like it."

Katie laughed. "I'm surprised to hear that. But glad."

"Eliza's been great to work with," Gabriel said.

Katie looked shocked but quickly covered her expression with a bland smile.

Eliza gasped and knocked over a container of pens and pencils beside the black ledger book. They rolled across the counter and dropped onto the wooden floor, one by one. Eliza cringed each time one hit the floor. She crouched and tried to gather them all, but she missed most of them. She squinted and felt around the worn wooden floorboards with her fingers until she found a few more. Then she rose, pushed them back into the pencil container and ordered them neatly. Gabriel could see that she had missed several pencils. He figured she must have lost her glasses and was too embarrassed to admit it, so he waited until she walked away before he leaned down to pick up the rest of the pencils for her.

* * *

Eliza's plan wasn't going as well as she had hoped. Maybe it wasn't the best idea to help *Gott* along… But after listening to Viola, Eliza figured she had to do whatever she could to grab Gabriel's attention so that she could be a *gut* influence on him. And if he fell for her in the process, well, that would be even better.

The only problem was that flirting and fawning over a man wasn't as easy as it seemed. She wasn't very good at fake-smiling, apparently. Most of the morning, Eliza was sure she had been grimacing instead, no matter how hard she tried. And all that hovering over him, showering him with home-baked goodies—it left her feeling foolish. How could Lydia and Sarah act that way without seeming ridiculous? Probably because they had the looks to go with their actions. It seemed to Eliza that pretty girls could get away with almost anything.

Eliza sighed and reached up to adjust her glasses for the hundredth time that day, then dropped her hand when she realized they weren't there. She had not noticed how often she pushed the frames up her nose until now.

Eliza needed to unpack a box of porcelain figurines depicting Amish buggies, windmills and red barns with Holstein cows. But when she ripped off the tape and pulled open the cardboard flaps, everything inside looked blurry. Eliza's prescription required progressive lenses to help her see both far away and close up, so without her glasses, she couldn't make out much at all. Eliza wished she could secretly slip her glasses on now, but she had been so committed to her plan that she had purposely left them at home.

Eliza carefully unpacked the box as best she could and arranged the figurines on a shelf beside a row of scented candles. She squinted at the arrangement and hoped everything looked all right before straightening up and stretching her back. She suddenly realized that she had not paid Gabriel any attention in the last hour. How could she ever compete with Lydia or Sarah when she was too busy working?

Eliza smoothed her hair to make sure every strand was tucked beneath her *kapp*, then marched across the store to the counter. Gabriel sat slumped over a stack of invoices. At least Eliza *thought* that was a stack of invoices, but she couldn't really be sure. Katie stood over him, pointing to something on one of the papers.

"I'm going to go get that lemonade I made

for you this morning, Gabriel," Eliza announced. She had stored the pitcher in the Millers' propane-powered refrigerator in their farmhouse kitchen to keep it cold. "Bet you could use another glass, ain't so?"

Gabriel grinned. *"Ya."*

When Eliza returned a few minutes later, she noticed a couple browsing in the shop, and she passed by them on her way to the counter. She gave Gabriel a big smile that she hoped didn't look like a grimace and made a show of pouring him a tall glass of lemonade. "Here you go." She handed the glass to him. "Now let me get you some of those peanut butter cookies I made. A big, strong man like you must have a *gut* appetite, ain't so?" Eliza could not believe she had just said that. But she was willing to do whatever it took to win Gabriel over. She smiled again, then added a little giggle for good measure, even though it sounded forced.

Gabriel shifted in his seat, and Eliza could sense he was embarrassed. Well, that made two of them.

"Not going to offer your bishop any?" a familiar voice said from behind Eliza.

She spun around so fast that some of the lemonade splashed onto her apron. "Bishop

Amos?" Eliza stepped closer and squinted. "I didn't recognize you."

"I've known you since the day you were born, and you don't recognize me?" He chuckled. Eliza couldn't make out his face but because his features were so familiar, she could imagine his sharp nose, rosy cheeks and wizened expression that always reminded her of a jovial gnome. She also knew the plump figure beside him must be his wife, Edna, because the blurry outline was taller than him. Bishop Amos was a small man, even though his personality was big.

"Sorry," Eliza said quickly. "Let me pour a glass for both of you." She wanted to sink into the floor. Eliza did not flirt. Ever. Or not until today, at least. And the one time she had tried it, she had gotten caught.

"We'll take some of those peanut butter cookies too," Bishop Amos said.

"Of course." Eliza felt her face heat up with shame. She knew she must be red as a beet.

"I'll take some too," Katie said.

Eliza flinched. She'd thought Katie was in the back, going over inventory, but she was standing behind Amos and Edna, where Eliza hadn't noticed her. That meant Katie had also heard Eliza flirting with Gabriel. *Could this get any worse?*

"Interesting figurines you're selling these days," Amos said as Eliza passed him a plate of peanut butter cookies.

"The new ones we just got in?" Katie asked as she reached for a cookie and a napkin.

"Ya," Amos said. He nodded toward the porcelain figurines that Eliza had unboxed earlier.

"I thought the red barn looked pretty cute in the catalog and—" Katie cut herself off midsentence as her eyes landed on the figurines.

Eliza frowned. Something was wrong, but she didn't know what.

"Eliza…" Katie stared at the figurines for a moment, then looked to Eliza, then back to the figurines. "Did you notice anything wrong?"

Eliza squinted at the display but couldn't make out any details.

Amos chuckled, walked over to the shelf, picked up a figurine, doubled back and held it up to Eliza. "Take a closer look," he said.

Eliza leaned closer to the object and gasped. It was a figurine of Santa Claus in a red swimsuit, riding a surfboard. "This is…not…" Eliza didn't know what to say. "I didn't realize."

Bishop Amos laughed. "I figured it was a mistake. Doesn't exactly fit with the shop's theme." He waved a hand over the shelves of Amish quilts, Mason jars of canned goods, crocheted place mats, hand-carved wooden toys, framed Bible verses and bins of fresh vegetables from the farm. "Sticks out like a sore thumb." Amos's laughter spread through the room, until everyone was having a good chuckle at Eliza's expense.

Eliza could not believe how foolish she had been. How could she have thought that Gabriel would be impressed with this nonsense? And—more to the point—what was wrong with wearing glasses, anyway? If Gabriel didn't think she was pretty enough with them on, then that was his problem.

She was so shaken by her behavior that the heavy pitcher of lemonade slipped from her hand, hit the counter and splashed its contents across Gabriel. He yelped when the cold liquid hit his chest. Eliza stared for a few beats. Then she quipped in a dry tone, "Sorry, looks like I missed a spot. A corner of your shirt's still dry. I'll have to do better next time."

The room was dead silent for a moment; then Gabriel burst into laughter. "Now, there's the Eliza I like."

There's the Eliza I like. The words flooded her in a wave of joy. And suddenly, she didn't care that she had embarrassed herself. It had been worth it to hear that Gabriel liked something about her—even though he meant it just as a friend. It would still be enough to obsess about for weeks to come.

Chapter Seven

Eliza wore her glasses to the shop the next morning. She swept inside in her usual manner: face serious, hands clasped in front of her, ready to work. Katie was running errands in town, but Gabriel was already seated at his usual place behind the cash register, his foot propped up on the cushion she had brought him the day before. He had a block of wood in one hand and a pocketknife in the other. He set them both down, brushed aside a small pile of wood shavings, and turned his attention to her. "Looking much better today," he said with a sly smile.

"Better?" Eliza frowned and pushed her glasses up her nose.

"*Ya.* Better."

Eliza snorted. "I don't look better—but I do *see* better, and that's all that matters."

Gabriel studied her for a moment, and Eliza could tell he was debating whether or not to say something. He shrugged. "They magnify your eyes."

"You think that's *better*?"

"Uh, *ya*." Gabriel shifted in his seat. Gone was the playful bravado he displayed around other girls. He seemed suddenly embarrassed. Vulnerable, even. "You have very pretty eyes. It's nice to see them better. And those big, round frames outline them really nicely. They kind of—I don't know…highlight them."

Eliza stood frozen, staring at him.

He gave a self-conscious grin and looked away. "Stop looking at me like that."

"You're not making fun of me?"

His attention shot back to Eliza. The smile was gone. "*Nee.* I wouldn't make fun of you for wearing glasses. What kind of person do you think I am?"

She shook her head. "I'm sorry. I just had to make sure. No one's ever…" She cleared her throat. The emotions roiling within her were too much. He liked the way she looked? He thought her eyes were pretty? She didn't know whether to shout or faint. "I have to get to work," she said.

A faint half smile curled Gabriel's lip. "No one's ever *what*, Eliza?"

"Nothing. Never mind."

The half smile stayed on his face, but his eyes were serious as he kept them on her.

Eliza swallowed hard. "No one ever told me I looked pretty in glasses before." A few beats passed before Eliza realized what she had said. "Not that you said I looked pretty. You said I have pretty eyes, which isn't really the same thing. I didn't mean to suggest—"

"You are pretty, Eliza. With or without glasses. But I like you with glasses better."

Eliza felt the strength go out of her knees. Gabriel King said she was pretty. With or without her glasses.

"Now you're embarrassing me," Gabriel said.

"What?" Eliza squeaked.

"The way you're staring at me. Have I said the wrong thing?"

Eliza fought to form proper words. "*Nee*, you said just the right thing, Gabriel."

Gabriel's face lit up.

Eliza didn't wait for him to say anything else. She fled to the other side of the shop to regain her composure. She had never experienced anything like this before and had no idea what to do.

Eliza created jobs to keep busy while hiding behind the long rows of shelves, waiting for her heart rate to slow back down. She even took the time to coordinate the scented candles by color. After she had regained her composure, Eliza strode back to the counter with her head held high. She refused to show how shaken she was by Gabriel's compliment. Ironically, after all the failed effort yesterday, now that she had actually managed to get his attention, Eliza had no idea what to do next.

Gabriel sat slouched over the counter carving the block of wood she had seen him holding earlier. The pocketknife he was using looked small in his big, calloused hand.

"If you can't find work to do, I can find some for you," Eliza said, then immediately cringed inside. She had not meant to sound so combative.

Gabriel smiled and slapped down the block of wood. "Now that's the Eliza I missed yesterday. Glad to see you're back."

"You're…glad?"

"*Ya.* I don't know what got into you yesterday, but I didn't like it."

Eliza wondered if she should say what she

wanted to and decided she couldn't hold back. "You like it when other women act that way."

Gabriel looked amused. "You think so?"

"*Ya.* Of course."

Gabriel leaned back in his chair. "Then why aren't I courting any of those women?"

Eliza opened her mouth to answer, but no words came out. She shook her head. "I... I don't know."

"Because I'm not impressed by all that."

Eliza narrowed her eyes. "What do you mean by 'all that'?"

"*Ach*, I don't know. Anything that doesn't seem genuine."

"And I seem genuine to you?" Eliza swallowed hard as she waited for the answer.

"You do today."

"You don't think I'm too bossy? Or too uptight?"

Gabriel chuckled. "Sometimes. But you're never boring." His expression turned serious. "Anyway, I don't think it's fair to call you bossy. I think you just know your own mind and aren't afraid to say so. Men act the same way, and people like it. They say it's decisive and bold. Why shouldn't they like it when you do the same thing?"

Eliza was floored. She had never thought of

that before. "You don't sound like anyone else I've ever met."

Gabriel took a deep breath and let it out slowly. "*Ya*, well, maybe that's because I don't belong here."

Eliza inhaled sharply. "Of course you belong here. How could you not? You're Amish."

Gabriel stared at her for a moment, eyes locked. She could sense an unseen sadness behind those eyes. Then his face changed, as if a curtain had been drawn. He grinned. "You'd miss me if I left, ain't so?"

"Stop making a joke of it," Eliza said. "This is serious."

"You're right." The grin stayed on his face, but there was no mirth in his eyes. "No one in Bluebird Hills would miss me."

"Gabriel." She gave him a level stare. "That's enough."

"Have you thought of another career? You'd make a great schoolteacher. You could quiet the entire classroom with just one look."

"Stop changing the subject."

"You're *gut*, Eliza. Can't get away with much around you."

"And you're used to getting away with a lot, ain't so?"

Gabriel shrugged.

"No one actually gets past your grins and compliments, do they?"

"They don't need to," Gabriel said. "There isn't anything beneath them."

"I don't believe that."

Gabriel stared at her. Silence stretched between them. Eliza didn't think Gabriel was going to respond. But he finally said, in a quiet voice, "You're the first not to, then."

"I don't believe that either."

Gabriel snorted. "I'd say you're lying, but I know you wouldn't. You didn't get the nickname Eliza the Perfect for nothing."

Eliza cringed. "Don't call me that."

"I didn't mean to insult you."

"But you did," Eliza said. "Every time I think there's more to you than appears, you say something like that." She shook her head, turned around and walked away, the name Eliza the Perfect ringing in her ears.

Gabriel watched Eliza storm across the shop. Why had he pushed her away? They were having a good conversation—a *really* good one—until she scared him by seeing what was underneath his carefully built facade. And then she insisted she wasn't the only one who could see beneath it. Did she really believe that he wasn't shallow and lazy? Didn't she know the entire community thought he was a slacker?

Of course, he'd given up over the last few years and played the part, so who could blame them? He shook his head and put away the woodcarving he had been working on. He had lost his motivation.

Gabriel pulled a paperback book from his coat pocket to occupy him instead. Better not to get too close to Eliza, anyway. Offending her was probably for the best. Otherwise, she might expect more from him than he could give.

Gabriel tried to concentrate on the words on the page, but every time he got to the end of a paragraph, he realized he hadn't read any of it. His eyes were going through the motions, but his mind was somewhere else. He turned down the corner of the page, closed the book and dropped it onto the counter with a thump. He may as well give up. Guilt was tickling the back of this mind, even though he was sure the best thing for Eliza was to keep her away from him.

And yet he just couldn't resist. The thought of her face when he called her that silly old nickname was too much. He could see the hurt sear right through her, no matter how hard she had tried to hide it. For all her toughness, Gabriel knew Eliza was a lot softer than people realized.

"Hey, Eliza," he called across the shop.

Silence.

"Eliza?"

A heavy sigh. Then footsteps thudded across the worn floorboards. Eliza appeared at the end of an aisle, hands planted on her narrow hips.

"Ah, just who I wanted to see."

"*Ya*, I guess so. You just called me."

She was still annoyed with him. That was certain sure. "Women usually like it when I joke around."

"I can't account for other women."

Gabriel smiled. "No, I guess not."

Eliza sighed through her nose. "Did you need something?"

"*Ya.*"

"What?"

"*Kumme* here and I'll tell you."

Eliza hesitated, then rolled her eyes and marched over to the counter. She stood on the other side from his chair, glaring down at him. "What do you need?"

"I need you to accept my peace offering."

"Oh."

Gabriel flashed a grin. "Not what you expected me to say?"

"Nee."

"I'm sorry I brought up the nickname. I shouldn't have done that." He picked up his paperback book and held it out to her. "Here. Take this."

She peered down the bottom of her glasses at the book as if it were an insect. "Why? What is it?"

"A *buch*."

"I can see that."

Gabriel noticed that her tone was softening. He was starting to win her over.

"A very *gut buch*. One of my favorites."

"You have a favorite *buch*? You read…for fun?"

Gabriel's grin widened. "Didn't think I knew how to read?"

"I didn't think you would care to read. For fun. You never did in school."

"That's because school assignments are boring. This is interesting."

Eliza's forehead crinkled in concentration as she slowly took the book from his hand. She held it cautiously, as if it might attack her. *"Wuthering Heights*. By Emily Brontë. What is this?" Eliza turned it over and scanned the back cover.

"It's a classic."

Eliza pursed her lips but opened the book and flipped through the first few pages as Gabriel watched. "I'm not sure Bishop Amos would approve."

Gabriel shrugged. "Maybe not. But the message is about how a lack of forgiveness and the need for revenge will destroy you. He'd approve of that."

"Hmm." Eliza studied the pages with narrowed eyes.

"I think you like to read, too," Gabriel said. "And I bet you've read secular books."

Eliza gasped, slamming the book shut. Her eyes rose to his. "How did you know?" She swallowed and added in a whisper, "It's my secret weakness."

Gabriel laughed. "*That's* your secret weakness?"

Eliza nodded, eyes wide. "*Mamm* would be very disappointed if she knew."

"What kind of books do you read?"

Eliza was silent.

"Come on, you can tell me. I promise I won't say anything to anyone."

Eliza stared at him, remaining silent.

"I promise."

She covered her face with her hands and whispered, "Amish romance."

"Amish romance?"

"Shh! Don't let anyone hear you!"

"Sorry." Gabriel swallowed a laugh and lowered his voice. "Eliza Zook, a sentimental romantic. Who would have guessed?

"No one, I hope." She leaned toward him and wagged her finger in his face. "And it better stay that way."

Gabriel held up his hands in surrender. "*Ach*, your secret's safe with me. Anyway, if I tell on you, then you might tell on me, and I don't want anyone to know I read this." He tapped the cover of *Wuthering Heights*. "It would not be *gut* for my image."

"And you want me to read it too."

"I think you might like it."

Eliza hesitated, then picked up the book. "I'll try it. But I'm not promising to finish it."

"Just give it a try. Then we can talk about it after you read it."

"Talk about it?"

"Ya."

"What for?"

"To share our thoughts and think more deeply about it."

A faint smile tugged at her lips.

"What?"

"I knew I was right about you," she said, then walked away.

Gabriel spent the rest of the day wondering what she meant by that—and why it made him so happy.

Word got around that Viola Esch's chickens had escaped the coop for the third time that week, and the community threw together an emergency work frolic to rebuild the coop before the chickens were lost for good. News traveled fast through Bluebird Hills, even without telephones or texts. Gabriel figured that without television and other diversions, folks must follow one another's lives a lot more closely than the *Englisch* did with all their newfangled distractions. Gabriel did have a cell phone since he was on his *rumspringa*. Youngies were allowed to take liberties with the *Ordnung* until they fully committed to the Amish way of life and were baptized. But even though Gabriel had more interesting things to do than listen to local gossip, the news reached him all the same.

After getting home from the shop and rushing through his after-work chores at *Aenti*

Mary's, he and Mary set out for Viola's. His aunt and a handful of other women would prepare a quick meal while the men did the repair work; then they would all enjoy dinner together. Gabriel was glad for the change of routine. He always welcomed change and excitement. Even better, Eliza would be there. That sent a little thrill up his spine, which was ridiculous because they had just spent the day together at the shop. Who would have ever thought he'd want to see more of Eliza?

He remembered the look on her face earlier that day, when he had guessed she had a secret passion for reading. Gabriel chuckled. Her expression had been priceless. He loved getting a reaction out of Eliza. And he had begun to suspect that she enjoyed his teasing—even though she still tried to put on a tough act around him. He didn't know any other woman who reacted the way she did. In fact, none of the other women he knew gave him a hard time about anything. They were too busy agreeing with him to try to impress him—which didn't impress him at all.

"What's so funny?" *Aenti* Mary asked. She turned to look at him from her place on the buggy's bench seat as he held the reins, eyes on the road ahead.

"Huh?"

"You just laughed out loud." She gave him a strange look. "Are you feeling *oll recht*?"

Gabriel smiled to himself. "Never better." He wondered if Eliza had started reading *Wuthering Heights* yet and what she thought about it if she had.

"You really didn't have to *kumme* today, you know," she said. "You won't be able to do much with that ankle of yours." She studied him for a moment. "It's not like you to go out of your way to work when you have a valid excuse."

Gabriel passed both reins into his left hand, slapped his right hand over his heart and gave his best wounded expression. "You hurt me, *Aenti* Mary."

"*Ach*, please," Mary said, not taking the bait. "It's almost as if you have an ulterior motive."

Gabriel didn't say anything, and he wondered how much Mary suspected. Surely no one would guess he was enjoying his time with Eliza Zook. It was *narrisch*, especially for him. Gabriel King was not the kind of man to enjoy talking about books with shy, uptight women.

If only people knew.

And that was the thing. Eliza *did* know. Somehow she had looked right past his bravado and had seen straight through to what was beneath.

Comet's hooves beat a steady rhythm across the pavement until they reached Viola's cream-colored farmhouse. She was watering a row of potted pansies on the front porch, saw them, straightened up and waved. Gabriel and Mary waved back as they pulled into her yard and parked on the grass. A small group of Amish trickled in behind them, waving and shouting greetings as they arrived. The job was relatively minor, so only a few families were needed, especially on such short notice.

Sadie and her father appeared over the hill, their dappled gray straining at the bit, mane and tail whipping in the wind. Bishop Amos and his *fraa*, Edna, followed close behind. The Millers pulled into the yard from the other direction, and Simon jumped from the buggy before it had come to a full stop. He clutched a Mason jar with holes poked in the lid, ready to catch small reptiles and amphibians when he wasn't helping the men.

Gabriel kept his eye on the road as he unhitched Comet and led her to Viola's pasture. His stomach leaped when he recognized Eliza's buggy rumbling over the hill. He tried not to grin and failed.

Simon tore across the yard to meet the Zooks' buggy, holding up the Mason jar for Priss to see. Gabriel watched as the little girl clambered out of the buggy. But Eliza shook her head and motioned toward the house before Priss could run off with her friend. The little girl's face fell, but she trudged obediently toward the front door. Amish children were expected to work alongside their parents. Play came second—if they had completed their chores first. Gabriel wondered if he would be able to maintain that level of discipline if he became a father. It would be hard not to let his *sohn* or *dochder* run free at a time like this, just to see them smile.

Ach, well, just one more reason why he didn't belong here.

Gabriel tarried beside the pasture, timing his walk to the chicken coop in order to run into Eliza. When their paths crossed, Gabriel waited until Lovina was just out of earshot and whispered, "Started reading the *buch* yet?"

Eliza's attention shot to Lovina, who strode ahead without noticing, then back to Gabriel. "Shh," she said. Then leaned closer. "*Ya*. I can't put it down. *Mamm* almost caught me because I was reading while I was taking the laundry off the line."

Gabriel chuckled. "How'd you manage that?"

Eliza shrugged. "It doesn't take a lot of concentration to pull down laundry. You just hold a *buch* in one hand and kind of scan it while you—"

"Eliza, *kumme*!" Lovina called over her shoulder. "Dinner won't cook itself, and these menfolk will be getting hungry soon."

"Coming, *Mamm*." Eliza hurried away without finishing her sentence. Gabriel watched her go, then realized he had been staring with a funny smile, mouth slightly agape. He snapped it shut and shook his head. What had gotten into him?

Gabriel headed toward the chicken coop. "What *gut* will you be with that ankle of yours?" Viola called from the porch.

"I'll be the comic relief," Gabriel said with a grin.

"Ach." Viola gave him a stern look as she watered the last of the potted pansies, then set down the green plastic watering can. "What would your father say to that?"

The air whooshed right out of Gabriel's lungs. Why did she have to bring his father into this? And why couldn't she be thankful he was here to help? People criticized him for not helping enough, and now they criticized him for helping. Gabriel wanted to say something but resisted the temptation. He didn't want to disrespect an elder, no matter how much she had hurt him. So he jammed his hands into his pockets and hobbled away.

Gabriel slouched on a stump beside a sawhorse, where he could take care of any job that could be done sitting down. He wasn't as much help as he would have been on two good feet, but he wasn't a complete waste of space, either—no matter what Viola or his father might say. Gabriel sighed as he sanded a rough wooden board. Viola didn't mean any harm—everyone knew that about her, but it didn't stop her words from cutting to the quick.

A short distance from Gabriel, the small group of men chatted and joked as they measured, hammered and sawed, the clatter of tools competing with the low drone of voices. Chickens squawked and clucked as the men invaded their space, feathers scattering into the air.

Inside, the women were making good things to eat in the kitchen. Cooking was a mystery to Gabriel. He had no idea how a handful of ingredients magically transformed into thick cream sauces, flaky pastry crusts and rich desserts. He only knew that he liked it. His gaze wandered from the sandpaper in his hand to the kitchen window. He could make out Eliza washing dishes behind the glass. She was always diligent, always on task. He appreciated that about her. She never slacked off, never made excuses. He watched as her hands flew across the pots and pans and her face kept that somber expression he had grown to love.

Love? Gabriel focused his attention back to the work at hand. Admired and liked. That's what he had meant. The word *love* had just been a strange, fleeting thought. He felt beads of sweat form on his forehead and wiped them away with his royal blue shirtsleeve. His collar felt too tight, so he tugged at it with a finger.

"You *oll recht*, Gabriel?" Amos shouted from where he lay sprawled across the roof of the chicken coop, a hammer in one hand.

"Ya," Gabriel said too quickly. "Of course."

"You look like you've taken sick all the sudden."

"Nee." Gabriel attacked the board he had been sanding with newfound vigor. "Never been better." He refused to look at the window again. But he couldn't keep his thoughts from straying in that direction, no matter how hard he tried.

Chapter Eight

Eliza tried not to look at Gabriel as he lined up with the men for dinner. She knew she would give herself away if she did. Her *mamm* picked up on everything. And Eliza was near-to-bursting with so much to say to Gabriel that she knew it would show on her face. So she kept her eyes down as she scooped chicken pot pie and macaroni and cheese onto plates and passed them out. Her hand faltered as she handed Gabriel his plate, but she managed to keep her eyes down as if he weren't there. She thought he paused for a moment, as though waiting for her to notice him, before moving on to grab a glass of lemonade. That had been her imagination, of course. Why would Gabriel want to get her attention when Sadie Lapp was standing nearby?

Sure, Gabriel had explained that he liked Eliza and even thought she was pretty. But he'd be *narrisch* not to prefer Sadie. Sadie was one of the prettiest women in Bluebird Hills. She had golden blond hair, rosy cheeks and light blue eyes that sparkled with personality. And as if that wasn't enough, Sadie was a talented artist. She was a free spirit like Gabriel, and Eliza had always thought they would make a perfect couple. A lot of people did, in fact. It seemed that it was only a matter of time before they ended up together.

Eliza snuck a peek at Gabriel as he passed by Sadie, who was pouring lemonade into glasses. He barely seemed to notice her as he picked up a glass and kept walking. Interesting. Eliza began to imagine what Gabriel and Sadie's life together would be like. They would always be laughing and joking, and pushing the limits of the *Ordnung* but somehow managing to get away with it. They would understand each other. They would entertain each other and never grow bored.

Eliza, on the other hand, would probably put Gabriel to sleep if he ever asked her out on a buggy ride. He would be so bored of her somber, sensible comments that he would doze off while holding the reins.

"Not going to feed your bishop?"

Amos's voice jerked Eliza's attention back to the present. "What?" She saw that they had run out of plated food for the last man in line. "*Ach*, sorry. My head was in the clouds."

"That's not like you, Eliza," Amos said.

"*Nee*. It most certainly is not." She scooped out a generous serving of chicken pot pie while refusing to give another thought to Gabriel or Sadie.

Until she heard Sadie's clear, strong laugh from across the kitchen. She motioned to Gabriel and he walked over to her, listened to her say something, and laughed along with her. Then they headed outside together, toward the picnic tables beneath Viola's old oak tree. Eliza tried not to look, but her eyes went to the window against her will. Sadie and Gabriel settled onto benches across the table from one another.

Eliza wondered how long she could hide in the kitchen. After the hope that Gabriel had given her earlier that day at the shop, it was too painful to be confronted with reality. How foolish she had been to think that he could ever feel *that way* about her. He may have meant it when he said she was pretty, but he had said it to spare her feelings. He was being thoughtful in the way a big brother would be. That's the kind of person he was—thoughtful and kind to people whom others would overlook. People like her. She was nothing more than a charity case to him.

Even so, the thought that he had been kind to her simply for the sake of being kind only made her love him more. The emotion sat in her chest like a stone, heavy and warm but achingly sharp around the edges.

"Kumme," Lovina said.

Eliza tore her attention from the window.

"I can't imagine what's gotten into you," Lovina said. "You're a million miles away today."

"Ya," Eliza said softly. "I am."

Lovina clucked her tongue. "Well, *kumme* back to reality because Priss is already outside with Simon, and who knows what trouble they might be getting into?"

"Simon's a *gut* boy," Eliza said as she served a plate for herself. The chicken pot pie was almost gone, but she managed to scrape a small portion off the sides of the casserole dish.

"Ach, he may not mean any harm, but he gets into trouble all the same," Lovina said.

"Remember that time he brought the frog to our house when we were hosting the church service?" Eliza smiled at the silly memory. There had been a minor incident when the animal escaped and Simon chased him across the living room—straight past Amos while he was in the middle of preaching—but no real harm had been done.

Lovina scowled. "You're only proving my point. Now hurry up, *ya*?"

Eliza sighed. *"Ya."* She plopped a hefty serving of macaroni and cheese onto her plate, grabbed a glass of lemonade and trudged after her mother. She didn't want to sit near Gabriel and Sadie, but Sadie waved her over as soon as she trotted down the back steps. Lovina headed to the other picnic table to sit with the older folks, and Eliza settled onto the bench beside Sadie. Sadie was always so friendly and upbeat that it was impossible to dislike her, even though she was a perfect match for Gabriel. She grinned at Eliza and nodded toward Priss and Simon, who sat on the ground with their backs propped against the big oak tree. "They're so cute together," Sadie said.

"Ya," Eliza said. "Until they stomp through the mud and Priss comes home with a stained dress and lost *kapp*." Eliza cringed as soon as the words came out of her mouth. Why did she

sound just like her mother? She knew better, and yet she kept falling into the same pattern.

Sadie looked at her for a few beats, managed a weak smile and turned back to Gabriel. Eliza could tell Sadie didn't approve of her killjoy attitude. Well, the truth was, Eliza didn't approve of it herself, as silly as that sounded. Maybe she did a few weeks ago, but since she'd been spending so much time with Gabriel, his carefree attitude had rubbed off on her. Not enough to change her ways, but just enough to make her want to stop and enjoy life a little—or let Priss enjoy it, at least.

"It's a beautiful evening, isn't it?" Sadie said wistfully. She propped an elbow on the table, rested her chin in her hand and stared out over the pastureland beyond Viola's yard. Long rays of golden sunlight swept over the lush spring grass and rolling hills. Birds darted across a cloudless sky tinged with pink as the horses grazed in the distance. "It's so perfectly still…" Sadie murmured. "You feel like you could just float away into the sky, with all that pink and gold."

Eliza adjusted her glasses and looked into the sky. The colors were pretty enough, but they didn't make her feel like floating. The thought would have never occurred to her. "I don't know why I'd want to float away when I have a perfectly good bench right here to sit on," Eliza said.

Sadie and Gabriel erupted in laughter. Eliza frowned and looked down at her plate. "I don't know why that's so funny. I think wanting to float away is a funnier thought."

Sadie grunted in agreement. "It is, I suppose. I just laughed because you're so sensible. We think so differently that it tickles me."

Eliza dared a quick glance at Gabriel. He was already looking at her, his dark eyes warm. "I was laughing because I was thinking the same thing as you," Gabriel said.

Eliza stiffened. "You were?"

"*Ya.* I appreciate the things Sadie says, but I don't always understand."

"*Nee*, you two are just alike, ain't so?"

Gabriel and Sadie turned their attention to each other. Sadie tapped her finger against her cheek, her chin still resting in her hand. "Hmm. Maybe." She shrugged.

"Too much alike," Gabriel said.

Sadie smiled and an understanding passed between them. Eliza caught the look and wondered how close those two really were. Were they already walking out together? Amish couples didn't advertise their courtships and often surprised the community when they announced their engagements. The thought shot through her like a red-hot spear. Eliza pushed her plate away and leaped up from the picnic table. "I've got to go."

Gabriel frowned. "You haven't finished eating yet."

"I have work to do at home. And it's already so late. The sun has set and it's Priss's bedtime soon, and…" Eliza moved back from the table. Her leg caught on the bench as she tried to step over and back. She lost her balance and threw her arms out, flailing at the air, as Gabriel scrambled to catch her. He leaped onto his good leg, managed to balance himself and grabbed her arm with a warm, firm grip.

"Steady, now. You *oll recht*?"

"*Ya*. Of course." She pulled away from him before adding, *"Danki,"* in a terse voice. She kept her face steady and blank. But inside, her entire body was shouting. Gabriel had not let her fall. He had rescued her. She turned away before she exposed her emotions and hurried to collect Priss.

Eliza tried to forget his touch. But long after she drove away from Viola's house, she could still feel the warm imprint of Gabriel's hand on her arm, burning into her skin.

* * *

The next day, Katie had to help Levi with another calving, leaving Gabriel and Eliza on their own in the shop. "So," Gabriel asked with a sly smile as soon as Katie headed for the barn, "what do you think of *Wuthering Heights*?"

Eliza looked down.

"Aha!" Gabriel pointed a finger at her. "I knew it! You like it."

Eliza groaned. *"Oll recht*, I admit it. I like it."

"What do you like about it?" Gabriel asked.

"I know who the bad guys are. The *buch* is pretty straightforward about that, which is *gut*. I like things to be clear."

Gabriel laughed. "It isn't supposed to be straightforward. It's supposed to be nuanced, complicated."

"Bah. I know a bad guy when I see a bad guy."

Gabriel laughed again. "See, this is what I like about you, Eliza. You aren't complicated. You see things for what they are, pure and simple."

Eliza frowned and pushed her glasses up her nose. "And you like that?"

"Ya." His expression turned serious. Eliza

felt a connection between them and had to look away.

"Is there something you want to say to me, Eliza? Because it's not like you to hold back."

She was silent.

"Eliza." Gabriel said her name so firmly yet gently that it made her heart quiver.

A few more beats passed. Eliza could feel Gabriel's eyes on her.

"*Ach*, fine," Eliza finally said. "You're right. I'd rather come right out and say it. I'd like to know what's going on between you and Sadie. Yesterday I realized that, well, you might already be a couple. You *are* just right for each other, ain't so?"

Gabriel didn't answer right away, and Eliza slowly raised her eyes to his. He lifted his eyebrows. "Just right for each other, huh?"

"*Ya.* Everyone knows it."

"And why would you think that?" Gabriel had an amused glint in his eye that confused Eliza.

"Not just me—*everyone*," Eliza said. Everyone except Viola, that is. But Eliza was beginning to doubt the elderly woman's suggestion that she and Gabriel were a good match.

"Why would 'everyone' say that about us?"

"Because it's obvious."

"Please explain." Gabriel crossed his arms and leaned back in his chair, awaiting her response with that smug grin that irritated Eliza *and* made her want to kiss him, as contradictory as that was.

"You're just alike. She's a free spirit and so are you. Neither one of you wants to be pinned down or told what to do. You need freedom from rules, from… I don't know." Eliza threw up her hands. "I can't explain it, because I'm not like that. I just know that she pushes the boundaries, same as you. And she's always joking and grinning, same as you. You're like two peas in a pod." Eliza hesitated, then added in a quieter voice, "And she's the prettiest girl in Bluebird Hills."

"Beauty is in the eye of the beholder," Gabriel said in a voice that was equally quiet and serious. He looked like he wanted to say more but hesitated and left it at that. "As far as us being alike, *ya*, I guess we are—in some ways, at least."

"In most ways," Eliza said.

"*Ach*, I don't understand a lot of what she says or does." Gabriel made a dismissive motion with his hand. "I respect her and her artistic talent—I don't have a problem with her art, like some people do—but I don't really get it."

Eliza straightened up. "You don't?"

"*Nee*. I'd rather have a good, straightforward picture of a landscape. Give me a nice red barn with a Holstein cow in the background. I can understand that. There's substance to it. I don't want to see a bunch of wavy lines and have to figure out what it's supposed to mean."

"You took the words right out of my mouth." Eliza grinned so wide that it made her face ache.

"I've never seen you smile so big before, Eliza."

"I've never had someone say exactly what I feel before, Gabriel."

Their eyes locked for a moment, and Eliza could feel the connection between them once more. Her mouth went dry, and she dropped her eyes. Blinking rapidly, she took off her glasses and began to wipe the lenses. She needed something to do, something to distract her, because the feelings welling up inside her were building like a tidal wave. She was afraid what might happen if she let them go. "But you're alike in other ways, ain't so? You both like to push the boundaries. You both need freedom. That would still make you a *gut* couple."

Gabriel laughed and shook his head. "*Nee*, that would make us a terrible couple."

Eliza's attention shot from the glasses in her hands to Gabriel. She squinted to make out his expression, then shoved her glasses back on to see him better. "What do you mean?"

"I don't want to be with someone like me. I want to be with someone who fills in all the spaces I can't fill in, someone who balances me."

Eliza released a breath she didn't realize she had been holding. "But that would mean..." She looked down. The question hung in the air like a soap bubble, so fragile that Eliza was afraid it would burst before she learned the answer.

"Ya." Gabriel reached out, gently placed his finger beneath Eliza's chin and raised her face to look at him. "That would mean that I like your predictability and sensibility." He stared at her, and Eliza's heart beat so fast she thought her chest might explode.

"It makes me feel safe. *You* make me feel safe."

Eliza felt moisture well in her eyes. She made Gabriel feel safe. Because of who she was. Boring, predictable, sensible. He *liked* that. He liked her for *her* and not for anything else.

It was all she had ever wanted and more than she had ever dreamed.

Chapter Nine

Gabriel stared into Eliza's eyes. She looked so beautiful—gazing up at him, blinking with what looked like joy and confusion. He wanted to take her in his arms and tell her that he wanted to feel safe with her forever. He wanted to kiss her. The moment was perfect.

But he couldn't. He had no future here with the Amish. No future with a good, upright woman like Eliza Zook. He had told her the truth. She deserved to know how he really felt. But that was all he could give her. And yet…

The doorknob rattled, the door swung open and the bell rang out as Simon and Priss ran into the shop. Gabriel pulled back from Eliza. She gasped. Her face turned a deep shade of red as the children raced across the floor and nearly collided with the counter when they reached Eliza and Gabriel. "Do you have snacks?" Priss asked.

"Katie's in the barn and said she can't get us anything right now," Simon added.

Gabriel watched as Eliza regained her composure. She pushed her glasses up the bridge of her nose with a slender forefinger, blinked a few times and then nodded. "*Ya.* I have something here for you." She walked behind the counter and reached into one of the shelves beneath it. Gabriel could feel her closeness as she stood beside him, shifting cardboard boxes and office supplies aside. He could not believe how close he had been to kissing her.

His feelings were getting out of control, and he needed to make sense of them before he went too far. If anything happened between Eliza and him, he would be obligated to stay and commit to her. He had been planning to leave for years; he just hadn't gotten up the courage to do it yet. If he got too entangled with Eliza, time would run out and he'd be stuck for good.

Maybe it would be worth it.

Gabriel frowned. No. He would fail her, for sure and for certain.

"Here," Eliza said as she pulled out a tin from the back of the shelf. "Molasses cookies."

Priss squealed and Simon leaped into the air.

Eliza smiled and handed them each two. They devoured them quickly. "Can we go outside and play now?" Priss asked before licking a crumb from her finger.

Simon looked up with big solemn eyes magnified by his thick glasses. Eliza's eyes flicked to the window. "*Nee.* It's raining out there." A steady patter of rain drummed against the tin roof and splashed into puddles throughout the farmyard.

Simon and Priss deflated.

"You can sit at the counter with Gabriel and play quietly," Eliza said. "I have some paper and pens, so you can draw."

Priss nodded. "I shouldn't get my dress muddy, anyway," she said. But her disappointed expression did not match her words.

"*Ya.*" Eliza gave a decisive nod, then turned to Gabriel. "Do you mind keeping an eye on them while I go over inventory?"

"Don't mind at all," Gabriel said with a grin. "We'll find a way to have fun inside."

Eliza was surprised to hear giggles and snorts of laughter while she worked. She didn't expect the *kinner* to be having that much fun. When she emerged from the back room to check on them, the paper and pencils she had laid out were untouched. Instead, Gabriel was gesturing and whispering to them. Then he leaned back, grinned and delivered a punch line that made both children erupt into laughter.

"What's so funny?" Eliza asked as she peered around the doorway.

"You wouldn't think it's funny," Priss said.

"She's probably right," Gabriel said with a sly glint in his eye.

Eliza rolled her eyes.

"Can we go out and play now?" Simon asked.

"Please?" Priss added.

Eliza glanced out the window. There was still a steady drizzle of rain with no sign of letting up; low-hanging clouds stretched over them like a damp, gray blanket. In the distance, the emerald green grass in the empty pastureland glistened with moisture. Water droplets dripped down fence posts and the spring buds on the crab apple trees. "Not even the horses are out today," Eliza pointed out. "And besides, you don't want to get your dress muddy, remember?"

Priss heaved a heavy sigh but nodded in agreement.

Gabriel looked from Eliza to the children, then back to Eliza. He hesitated, then said,

"Why don't you *kinner* go see if the quilts need refolding. That would be a *gut* help. Sometimes people unfold them when they're browsing."

"Okay." Simon and Priss hopped off their wooden stools and trotted over to the quilt display at the front of the shop.

Gabriel nodded for Eliza to come closer. She walked over to him. "Why don't you let them go out to play?" Gabriel asked in a low voice. "What can it hurt?"

Eliza frowned. "You heard Priss say she doesn't want to get muddy."

Gabriel scratched his chin. "I know her nickname is Priss—"

"Because she's so prissy," Eliza finished for him.

"*Ya.* That's what people say." Gabriel glanced across the shop to the quilt display, then back at Eliza. He leaned closer. "But is she actually the prissy one?"

Eliza's eyebrows slammed down. "What is that supposed to mean?"

Gabriel put a finger underneath his collar and tugged. The room felt hot and stuffy all of a sudden. "I mean, maybe she's just acting the way she thinks you want her to act. Maybe she isn't that prissy at all. Seems to me like she wanted to go out and play in the rain, but she wanted to please you more. Maybe she's just trying to be like you."

Eliza stared at Gabriel.

"I'm sorry if I said too much. I have a habit of doing that."

Eliza kept staring at him. Gabriel wasn't sure what to expect, but he suspected it would not be good. He had really overstepped this time. He only wanted to help, but he should have known better than to say something critical about Eliza's parenting. "You're a *gut* mother," he added hastily. "A very *gut* mother." He held up his hands in a gesture of supplication. "But we all miss something sometimes. Nobody's perfect, ain't so?"

"Nee," Eliza said in a terse voice. "Nobody's perfect."

"It's not a big deal."

"It might be." A look of vulnerability flickered across Eliza's face. Gabriel had never seen that expression on her before. "I think I…" Eliza furrowed her brow and looked down.

Gabriel put a hand on her shoulder. She felt thin and delicate beneath his rough, calloused palm. "It's *oll recht*."

She shook her head. "I think I may be passing down the traits that bother me most about *Mamm*."

"Go on," Gabriel said softly.

"She likes everything to be perfect. So I've always tried to be perfect. And I guess I've put that pressure on Priss too. She's too careful for a child her age. You're right—she should be outside getting dirty. I just…" Eliza shook her head again. "I don't know. There're a lot of layers. The pressure to live up to *Mamm's* expectations, the pressure to be a *gut*-enough *mamm* in the eyes of the community, especially after Rebekah left the way she did. *Mamm* carries a lot of shame from that. She feels—I guess we *both* feel—that we have to be extra careful to show everyone that we are *gut*, reliable Amish."

Gabriel gave her an encouraging nod. He had never heard Eliza open up like this. The moment felt so tender and so real that he didn't want to speak and risk ending it.

"And there's always that fear in the back of our minds that Priss will go the same way as her *mamm*. Her biological *mamm*, I mean. It's been so hard losing my sister—not just because I miss her every day, but because I know she's cut off from her family and her faith. It's almost too much to bear." Tears welled in Eliza's eyes, and she quickly swiped them away. "So, anyway, I suppose we've put too many restrictions on Priss. It just seemed safer that way."

Gabriel waited until he was sure she was finished speaking. He knew what he wanted to do, but he wasn't sure how she would react. He decided to go with his instincts. He really couldn't resist comforting this woman he had come to care for and admire. So he quietly took her hands in his. Her eyes shot up to his in surprise.

"I'm so sorry that your sister is shunned." He let the words sink in before continuing. "And I understand why you've reacted the way you have. I can only imagine how difficult it's been." He paused again. "But I'm afraid that being too hard on Priss might push her away in the long run."

Eliza nodded.

"Maybe Lovina was too hard on Rebekah? Maybe she expected too much?"

"I don't know anything about *kinner*, so I'm not trying to tell you what to do. You're Priss's *mamm*, and you know what's best for her. But I do know…" Gabriel shifted his weight from one foot to the other. Feeling the emotion building up, everything in him shouted not to tell Eliza how he really felt inside. He forced himself to push through for Eliza's and Priss's sakes. "I do know what it's like when a parent expects too much from you and how much that hurts. My *daed* was mighty quick to criticize me, no matter how hard I tried. Nothing was ever *gut* enough for him. And when I wasn't *gut* enough, he just set more rules that were impossible to follow." He quickly squeezed her hands. "I'm not comparing you to my *daed*— you're not hard on Priss like he was on me. I'm just letting you know that, in my experience, being too restrictive only drives a child away in the end."

Eliza let out a long breath. "Do you think it's too late? Have I already pushed her away?"

"Nee." Gabriel shook his head. "Of course not. But maybe you could start easing up a little. Let her play outside more, take some risks, allow her to be a child."

"I'll try. But it's going to be hard."

"Maybe I can help." Gabriel tightened his grip on Eliza's hands. They felt warm and soft beneath his fingers.

"I'd like that."

Gabriel flashed his signature grin. "You sure? Because that means I'm going to send her outside to play."

"Ach." Eliza clamped her eyes shut as though in pain, but she nodded in agreement.

"Gut." Gabriel gave Eliza's hands a final squeeze and released them. "Hey, *kinner,"* he

shouted across the shop. "Eliza says you can go outside and play."

Both children tore across the shop. Priss collided into Eliza and wrapped her arms around her *mamm's* waist in a tight hug. *"Danki!"*

Simon pumped his fist in the air. "Let's go!" The two children raced toward the front entrance, shouting and laughing, and were gone with a quick bang of the door.

Eliza was shaken. She had not expected such wisdom or support from Gabriel. He seemed to understand her. *Really* understand her. What a rare and wonderful gift that was.

After the children ran out to play, she wasn't sure how to react to what Gabriel had shared about his father. He seemed withdrawn and embarrassed, so she didn't want to press him by bringing it back up. But every word he had said burned in her mind.

She had met Gabriel's father. Before Gabriel's mother died, the family had lived in the Bluebird Hills church district, and Gabriel had attended the same one-room schoolhouse as Eliza. After his mother passed away from cancer, Gabriel's father bought a farm in another nearby church district. Gabriel had moved with him but eventually moved back to live with his father's younger sister, Mary. Eliza had not known why, but she noticed that he never mentioned his father. His father never came to visit him, and Gabriel never visited him, though he only lived twenty miles away. While inconvenient, it would have been easy to hire an English driver to make the trip. She had always wondered what had happened between them. Now she knew. She didn't know all the details, but she knew enough to understand Gabriel a lot better.

Turns out, they were not so different after all. They had both spent their lives trying to be *gut* enough.

Eliza wondered why Gabriel reacted by rebelling instead of overachieving like she had. It was the same question she had asked herself a million times about Rebekah and herself. She thought about it as she studied Gabriel from across the room. He was flipping through a catalog, marking items that needed reordering. His hair was tousled in that adorably careless way she loved. His lips moved as he sang under his breath, and he tapped his good foot. She wondered what he was singing. Something secular and forbidden, probably.

"Stop watching me," he said without looking up, then grinned.

"*Ach*, I'm not watching you."

"*Ya*, you are."

Eliza blushed and turned away, but she couldn't keep a smile from creeping up her face. Her hands still felt warm and secure from his touch earlier. She didn't know what he might do or say next, but she couldn't imagine anything better than holding his hands and gazing into his soft green eyes. Even though he had told her things that were painful to hear, he had delivered the message with such love that she had been able to accept it.

Eliza had never dreamed that Gabriel would notice her, much less treat her with such thoughtful consideration. First, they had become friends—which was a miracle in itself—and now they had passed that unspoken line into something more.

Gabriel's chair scraped against the floor, and she glanced back over at him. He pulled himself up and grabbed his crutches. "Going to go check on the *kinner*."

"But your ankle." Eliza frowned. "You should stay off it."

"*Nee*, it's a lot better. I'll be *gut* as new soon."

"That's *gut* to hear." But Eliza couldn't help feeling a small stab of disappointment. As soon as Gabriel's ankle healed, he would go back to working on the farm.

Gabriel hobbled across the floor, grabbed his straw hat from the hook by the door, pushed it onto his head and strode outside. Eliza moved over to the window to watch him cross the porch, shuffle down the steps and navigate the farmyard until he reached Priss and Simon. A light mist of rain settled on Gabriel's shirt and hat, but he didn't seem to mind. Instead, he flashed a grin and joined their game. Eliza didn't know what they were playing, but she could tell from the smiles and shouts that they were all having fun. Her heart warmed as she watched.

It might not seem like it on the surface, but Gabriel would make a very good father. After today, she let herself dare to hope that he might become one sooner than anyone expected.

Gabriel flashed a mischievous grin and slapped a puddle of water, splashing Priss. She whooped and splashed him in return. They kept splashing each other and laughing loudly enough that Eliza could hear them inside the shop.

Yes, Gabriel would make a very good father.

Chapter Ten

Priss chattered away at the table as Lovina served helpings of mashed potatoes, green beans, meatloaf and sliced peaches. She only paused long enough to stuff a bite of food into her mouth and chew. Then she would swallow and get right back to finishing her sentence. Eliza felt a happy glow as she watched Priss. The little girl's round cheeks were rosier than ever. And the way she squinted when she smiled was adorable.

Lovina looked down at Eliza's plate and pointed to it with her fork. "You're not eating?"

"*Ach*, I was just thinking," Eliza said.

"About what?" Lovina asked before Priss could get a word in edgewise.

Eliza breathed in, smiled and exhaled. "Mmm, just about how *gut* everything is right now. I feel so happy." Eliza realized that she couldn't remember the last time she had felt truly, genuinely happy. She used to feel a sense of satisfaction from completing her jobs and doing her duty each day—but not true happiness. Gabriel had woken something inside of her.

Lovina studied her daughter's expression for a moment, then looked away.

"What's for dessert?" Priss asked.

"Already finished?" Eliza asked with a smile.

"Uh-huh." Priss nodded and rubbed her tummy.

"I made a rhubarb pie." Lovina scooted out of her chair, rose from the table and walked over to the pie safe.

"Yay!" Priss clapped her hands.

"I don't know how you can eat anything else after that big supper you just ate," Lovina said as she opened the pie safe door, slid out the pie and grabbed a cake knife from the kitchen drawer.

"I worked up a big appetite today," Priss said. "We had lots of fun, me and Simon."

"That's *gut*," Lovina doubled back to the table and set down the pie with a gentle thump.

The sweet, tart smell of warm rhubarb filled the air. "What did you do?"

"Gabriel told us funny stories and made up funny songs. Then Simon and I went outside to play and then Gabriel came outside and splashed us. I splashed him back and he said I won."

Lovina's hand froze above the pie, and her knuckles whitened around the cake knife. "Gabriel King?" she asked.

Eliza's stomach dropped. She wished she could have warned Priss not to say anything. But that would have been too close to lying. Best to be open and face the consequences.

"*Ya*. He's nice, ain't so?" Priss reached over and helped herself to the slice of pie that Lovina had been in the process of serving. Lovina shot a look at Eliza. Eliza squirmed in her seat.

"Gabriel King is a lot of things, for sure and for certain," Lovina said vaguely.

Priss didn't seem to notice the tension that had entered the room. She was too busy shoveling rhubarb pie into her mouth. After a few bites, her lips and fingertips were coated in sugary goo. Eliza leaned over to dab Priss's mouth and hands with a napkin, grateful for any activity to distract her from Lovina's criticism. Priss wiggled away and took another big bite of pie.

Lovina said nothing more about Gabriel, and Eliza hoped that her mother would let the subject go. But as Lovina ate her pie, Eliza could sense the waves of disapproval wafting from her. The tight jaw and sudden silence gave her away. Eliza braced herself for whatever conversation her mother would spring on her as soon as Priss was out of earshot.

Eliza made it through dessert, cleaned the kitchen alongside Lovina and Priss, and tucked Priss into bed before her *mamm* cornered her. Eliza had taken a mug of herbal tea onto the porch and was rocking in the dark when the screen door whined opened and slammed shut, and footsteps padded across the painted-concrete floor.

Eliza wrapped her hands around her mug to draw comfort from the warm porcelain. The road that led to Main Street lay still and silent. Crickets chirped in the distance, and a dog barked somewhere far away. She closed her eyes, took a deep breath and let it out slowly. When she opened her eyes again, Lovina stood above her, hands on her hips, staring down. Her small, thin figure was silhouetted by the light of the half-moon that hung in the sky beyond the house. White moonlight filtered onto the porch and spilled across the side of Lovina's face, just enough to show that her features were pulled into a frown.

"Why don't you sit down, *Mamm*?"

Lovina heaved a dramatic sigh before shaking her head and settling into the rocking chair beside Eliza. She threw up her hands as soon as her bottom hit the seat. "What more can I do?"

Eliza kept her gaze straight ahead, toward the dim shapes of bushes and the dark outline of the bird feeder.

"Didn't I warn you?" Lovina waited for an answer. When none came, she tugged Eliza's sleeve. "Well, didn't I?"

"*Ya, Mamm.* You did."

"And now Priss is all tangled up in this, the poor lamb."

"You're overreacting. There was no harm in it."

"*Nee.*" Lovina shook her head. "It is not an overreaction to recognize that it's dangerous for my granddaughter to fall under that man's influence. He will bring trouble, for sure and for certain. His kind always does."

"What do you mean by *his kind*?" Eliza's voice sounded sharper than she had intended.

Lovina narrowed her eyes at Eliza. "Rebellious. Disrespectful of parents and of our ways. You can't let him teach Priss to be that way too."

"If you got to know him, you'd know Gabriel isn't like that at all."

Lovina snorted. "I know his father. *Ach*, he's a hard man, but he's a *gut* man. Gabriel moved away and left him alone—abandoned all his responsibilities. It isn't right. Now I hear talk that Gabriel is going to leave the Amish. He's already halfway in the *Englisch* world, with his fancy electronics and worldly ways. He has a laptop, you know. And I hear he listens to secular music and reads secular books." Lovina held up a hand, palm outward. "I know *youngies* are allowed some leeway during *rumspringa*, but Gabriel's has gone on far too long. He's not committed to our ways."

Eliza felt a surge of frustration, and the words flew out of her mouth before she could stop them. "First of all, being 'hard' is no excuse for mistreating a child. Men like Gabriel's *daed* hide behind that label all the time, and it isn't right. They shouldn't get away with it. If Gabriel's *daed* had treated him fairly and lovingly, Gabriel would never have moved out. And, *ya*, Gabriel is tempted by worldly living, but that's because he feels rejected by his *daed* and by our community. He's trying to figure everything out and needs some grace while he comes to closure with his past and learns how to move forward. If people like you would stop being so hard on him, then maybe he wouldn't feel the need to run away."

Eliza stopped for breath. She could not believe she had said all that. Never before had she poured out her true feelings to her mother with such force and honesty. Her face was flushed and hot, her hands sticky with sweat. Her heart thudded in her throat. She was afraid to keep talking, but it was too late to stop now. The floodgate had opened.

Lovina stared at her with a strange look on her face.

Eliza took a deep breath and plunged ahead. "I'll have you know that Gabriel has not been a bad influence on Priss. He's been a *gut* influence. In fact, he's been *wunderbar gut* for her. Haven't you noticed how much happier she is? She's smiling more. She's less anxious. She's taking risks. She's *living*. And it's because he's influenced us to loosen up and live a little. He says that if you overprotect and stifle your child, they're more likely to rebel than—"

"Stop," Lovina said. She said the word quietly, but her tone dripped with power. "I will not hear another word of this." Her face was pale, her jaw tense. "I cannot believe what's happened."

"Nothing has happened, *Mamm*. Gabriel—"

"Don't tell me anything else about that man. Something has happened—that much is painfully clear."

"Nothing but *gut* has happened!"

"You've fallen in love with him." The accusation hung in the still night air. "How could you?" Lovina shook her head and lowered her voice before repeating, "How could you?"

"Nee!" Eliza shook her head. "That's not true."

"Don't lie to me on top of everything else. I can see it by the way you talk about him, by the way you defend him. The look you get on your face."

"I'm not…" The sentence died on Eliza's lips. She could see in Lovina's eyes that she knew beyond a doubt. Eliza could not hide it anymore. "You should see him with Priss," Eliza said instead. "You'd understand."

"Nee. I will never understand this."

"He's not a bad man."

"Maybe not, but he's a dangerous man. He'll leave the Amish, and he'll tempt you and Priss to go with him."

"I don't think he's going to leave, *Mamm*. Not now. Not after we've become..."

"Become what, Eliza?"

Eliza swallowed hard. "Friends."

Lovina leaned closer to her daughter. "Not more than friends?"

"I—I don't think he knows that I love him. He couldn't know. He hasn't asked me to walk out with him. Not yet."

Lovina pulled back, closed her eyes and exhaled. "Thank *Gott* for that. We can still save you."

"I don't need saving, *Mamm*."

Lovina's eyes flew open. "You would break my heart? You would choose this man over me?"

"It wouldn't be like that."

"Don't be naive. That is exactly what it would be like."

Eliza didn't know what to say to that. She knew that no matter what she said, it wouldn't convince her mother. She tried to keep her breath even while her heart pounded and her hands clenched into fists by her sides.

"After what Rebekah did…" Lovina's voice broke. She swallowed before continuing, in a weak voice, "It would kill me, Eliza. Do you understand? It would kill me if he courted you, if he married you and he took you away." Lovina grabbed her daughter's arm. Her grip felt as tight as a talon. "Don't you see? I can't bear to lose you too. I can't bear it."

Eliza had never seen her mother like this before. She could see straight through her eyes and into the vulnerability and fear behind them. Eliza felt utterly shaken. Lovina's walls had crumbled, leaving a scared and pleading old woman. Eliza's heart twisted in her chest, torn between two loves.

"I won't do that to you, *Mamm*."

"You won't walk out with him? You'll stop speaking to him?"

"Isn't it enough to promise not to leave the Amish?"

"*Nee*. He'll influence you and change your mind." Her grip on Eliza's arm tightened.

"I can't stop seeing him. We work together."

"We can fix that."

"*Nee*. Please don't interfere." But Eliza looked into her mother's eyes and knew she could not deny her. Not when the pain from the loss of Rebekah was laid so bare. Eliza squeezed her eyes shut against the enormity of what she was about to say. *"Oll recht,"* she whispered. "I'll keep my distance."

"Oh, *danki*, Eliza!" Lovina grabbed Eliza's hand, drew it to her mouth and kissed it. *"Danki.* You won't be sorry. I promise. It's all for the best. You'll see."

But Eliza was already sorry.

Gabriel whistled as he unhitched Comet, gave her a good pat on the neck and led her to pasture. The sun shone brightly over the green fields and sparkled across the mud puddles from yesterday's rainstorm. The red wheelbarrow and big red barn looked brighter and more cheerful than usual. The sky seemed bluer, the world more vibrant. Gabriel felt more alive than he ever had before.

Was this what it felt like to be in love?

Gabriel wasn't sure what that was supposed to be like, but he did know he hadn't ever felt anything like this before, that was for certain sure. Not only did the world seem a happier, better place, but also his thoughts constantly turned to Eliza. He thought about her as he did his evening chores and when he drove his buggy down the long country roads of Bluebird Hills. He thought about her as he ate the eggs and bacon that Mary cooked for breakfast and as he stoked the fire in the woodstove. It was *narrisch*. But even odder was that he enjoyed being stuck on Eliza. Thinking of her made him feel happy and excited. He actually looked forward to going to work every day.

Gabriel wasn't ready to say that this was definitely love, but he knew it was *something*. And whatever that something was, it was changing him in ways he had never expected. He found himself making plans for the future—a future in Bluebird Hills. He daydreamed about taking over the family farm that his father owned. For the first time in his life, he wanted to put down roots. He wanted to be responsible.

He wanted to be like Eliza.

Gabriel patted the paperback in his pocket before hobbling up the steps and onto the front porch of the gift shop. As his crutches thudded against the floorboards, Gabriel noticed his ankle didn't hurt. He would be able to put weight on it soon. He was eager to be back up and about but didn't want to stop seeing Eliza every day. Maybe that meant it was time to ask Eliza to walk out with him.

She would say no. There was no way she would accept him. He wasn't even baptized, while Eliza had been baptized as soon as she was old enough. She had not waited at all—not even to have a *rumspringa with the other youngies*.

And yet they had laughed together, shared their feelings, connected over a book. They had held hands. Now Gabriel had brought another book for her to read and discuss. He grinned as he pulled open the gift shop door and heard the familiar ring of the bell overhead. If their conversation went well today... Well, maybe he would ask her to go on a buggy ride with him. That seemed like a good way to test the waters. The thought kept a goofy smile on his face as he made his way to his chair behind the counter. Nothing ventured, nothing gained. Of course, people would go wild when they heard he was walking out with Eliza Zook. That just made him smile even wider. Let them talk. If they didn't see the treasure she was, that was their loss. They should have made the effort to get to know her better.

He was so thankful he had.

"Gude Mariye!" Gabriel said when Eliza appeared from behind a row of shelves.

She stared at him for a moment, blinked rapidly, then dropped her eyes and said, "Good morning," in a quiet voice.

Gabriel frowned. "Everything *oll recht*?"

"*Ya.* Of course." Eliza pushed her glasses up her nose.

"You do that when you're worried or irritated."

"I do?"

"*Ya.*"

Eliza paused for a moment, then shook her head. "*Nee.* The frames just need tightening, that's all."

"Well, in that case, *kumme* sit." He patted the countertop beside him. "I've got something for you."

Eliza bit her lip and glanced from Gabriel to the empty chair next to his, then back at Gabriel. "*Ach*, I've got so much to do right now…."

"It'll only take a minute." He pulled the paperback from his pocket, dropped it onto the counter and grinned. "See what I brought you?"

Eliza adjusted her glasses and studied the cover. She did not return his smile.

Gabriel's grin faded as he watched her reaction. "You don't want to read it?"

"*Nee*—I mean, *ya*, I want to, it's just…"

"It's just what, Eliza?" Gabriel's face fell into a frown. What had happened to their easy camaraderie?

She looked at him with a blank expression. Seconds ticked by as Gabriel stared at her. Finally, she shook her head and said, "*Nee*, I don't want to read it. And I think it's best that we don't talk about books anymore…or anything else like that."

Gabriel felt like he had been punched in the gut. "What?"

Eliza took a small step back. Gabriel could sense that she was moving much farther away from him than that one small step. "You heard me," she said in a voice that was so quiet he could barely make it out.

"I don't understand. We had something real here. At least, I *thought* we did."

"We did."

"Just not anymore?" Gabriel asked.

She stared at him with hollow eyes and did not answer.

"What happened, Eliza?"

"I've been thinking about things. Last night I couldn't sleep, turning it all over in my head. Talking to you, reading new books, exploring new ideas…" She put up her hands, palms facing him. "It isn't a *gut* idea."

"Why not?" Gabriel didn't mean for the words to come out as hard as they did, but he could feel the rejection and disappointment coursing through his body with physical force.

"Because it leads to questions, and questions lead to—"

"You think I'm leading you astray? You think I'm a bad influence."

"Nee!"

Gabriel gave her a long, hard stare.

"Not exactly." Eliza dropped her eyes. She ran her finger along a crack in the butcher block countertop. "It's complicated."

"It doesn't have to be."

"There's Priss to consider…"

"Priss and I get along great. I've never seen her laugh and smile as much as she has recently."

Eliza didn't answer.

"Did Lovina put these ideas in your head?"

"Nee." Eliza furrowed her brow. "Well, at first she did. But then I thought about it. And the more I thought about it…" Her face took on a pleading look, as if she wanted to change the truth but couldn't.

"So you *do* think I'm a bad influence."

Eliza hesitated. "I've been so careful all my life, especially after Rebekah left. How can I risk breaking *Mamm's* heart? How can I risk choosing the wrong path because I listen to my heart instead of my head? I've seen where the heart takes you, and that can be a dangerous place."

Gabriel tried to form an argument and couldn't. All this time, while he had been falling for Eliza—and while he thought she was falling for him—she had been judging him. She still saw him as the rebellious ne'er do well, just like the rest of the church district. Just like his father.

"Gabriel?" Eliza stared at him with soft, pleading eyes magnified by her glasses. She looked so lost and vulnerable that he wanted to reach out and touch her face. He wanted to draw her to him, press her against his chest and whisper into her ear that everything would be all right.

But she didn't want that. She didn't even want to talk to him anymore.

"Is it true that you're planning on leaving the Amish like everyone says?" she asked, her brown eyes steady on his.

He had changed his mind about that. Until now... Gabriel snorted and shook his head. "Not much to keep me here now, ain't so?"

Eliza inhaled sharply. A flicker of hurt passed over her face; then she regained her composure and gave a somber nod. She seemed miles away from him, and Gabriel could sense that she had closed herself off again, back to the way it had been when they first began working together. "I don't suppose there's anything I can say to change your mind."

Gabriel gave Eliza a level stare. He could hear her breathing in the still, tense room. The pulse in her neck jumped in time with her heartbeat.

"Nee," he said. "I don't suppose so." *Not anymore.*

Eliza nodded again and exhaled. "I guess that's that, then."

"I guess so."

They stared at each other for a moment before Eliza broke eye contact. She looked down, smoothed her apron and turned away. "I have work to do," she said before disappearing behind a display rack of colorful quilts.

Chapter Eleven

Eliza held her breath as she escaped. The shop felt too stuffy, the air too hot.

Her eyes stung and her heart pounded in her throat.

What had she done?

Eliza managed to make it to the other side of the quilt rack before the tears broke loose. She pressed the back of one hand to her mouth to push back the sobs and braced the other hand on a shelf to steady herself. She would not cry. She would not. Eliza Zook did not cry.

And yet tears were streaming down her face.

Waves of emotion swelled within her and overflowed against her will. Year after year, she had gone through her days with steady resilience. She did not complain. She did not question. She did not fall apart.

So what was happening to her?

Had Gabriel shaken her so badly that the strength she had built up over all these years had shattered? She heard a thump and a sigh, and could imagine Gabriel perfectly, even though the shelves and quilt rack blocked the view. He was settling his foot onto the crate with the embroidered cushion. A page turned in the silent air, and she knew he was reading the book she had refused to take. Eliza wished she had explained better. She wished she had told him how much she wanted to read the book and hear his thoughts on it.

But what good would that have done? Her mother had been right. Gabriel was going *Englisch*. Maybe that was why Eliza could not control her emotions right now and why the tears would not stop flowing down her face. Eliza had been so sure that Gabriel wasn't the wayward man that people accused him of being. Even when her mother had lectured and pleaded the night before, Eliza had still had faith in him.

The doubt had come during the long, dark night, after she had blown out the kerosene lamp and silence fell over her bedroom. Thoughts of the future had pressed against her like low-lying storm clouds as she struggled to fall asleep. The fear had returned again and again, no matter how hard she tried to push it away; if Lovina was right, then Eliza would be guilty of taking two souls down the wrong path in addition to destroying her mother. Eliza had to think of Priss and not just herself. She could not risk that sweet, innocent girl's faith.

Eliza had still had a small, dim hope that Gabriel would fight for her this morning. If only he had insisted that he would stay in Bluebird Hills, that he was committed to the Amish way. But instead, he had given voice to her worst fears.

He was leaving.

Just like Lovina said.

Eliza leaned into a quilt that hung at eye level to muffle the sound of her crying. The soft, colorful cloth felt comforting and familiar against her skin. Then she realized that she might stain the fabric with her tears and jerked away. She threw up her apron and buried her face in it, shoulders heaving as she sobbed in silence. She was fighting so hard to keep her breath steady, to not make a sound as the tears rolled down her cheeks. She could not let Gabriel know that he had broken her heart. These happy, carefree days in the shop had meant nothing to him. They had only been a fantasy, nothing more. Nothing real.

Eliza had known better than to believe in dreams. She had given them up long ago. Gabriel had been her one indulgence beyond her beloved romance novels. But even those had been about him. No matter who the hero was, she had always imagined Gabriel's handsome face, with its splash of freckles, that playful grin and tousled, careless hair. He had always been her sweet, impossible dream. Until these last few weeks, when they'd formed an actual friendship that had given her hope for more...

Now she could only hope that Gabriel left soon. The longer he waited, the more it would hurt. Better to rip off the Band-Aid and get it over with.

Would he even bother to say goodbye? Had any of their conversations meant anything to him? Or had he just seen her as silly old stuck-up Eliza the whole time, same as everyone else?

Eliza decided she had given in to her emotions long enough. She dabbed her eyes with her apron, took a deep breath and then smoothed her hair and dress. Time to get on with it. She could not face seeing Gabriel, so she busied herself in the back of the shop, dusting shelves and sweeping. The minutes ticked by in agonizing slowness as she imagined Gabriel on the other side of the room, sitting alone, hurt by her judgment of him.

Eliza reminded herself that he was planning to leave the faith, proving her judgment right.

And yet she knew how thoughtful and introspective their conversations had been. She knew how sweet he had been with Priss. She still believed he had a good heart, no matter what other people said.

But even a good heart could choose the wrong path and go astray. Rebekah had a good heart too.

The sound of hoofbeats and the crunch of buggy wheels on gravel grabbed Eliza's attention. She propped the broom against the back wall and stretched her back, thankful for the distraction of customers. But when Eliza moved over to the window and peeked outside, she saw her mother striding toward the shop, arms pumping as she walked, her expression set in a determined grimace. Eliza braced herself as she went to meet her at the door.

"Where's Katie?" Lovina asked as soon as she crossed the threshold.

"In the kitchen, canning the farm's spring produce to sell in the shop."

Lovina gave a quick nod, turned on her heels and marched back out the door.

"Hello, Lovina," Gabriel managed to say before the door swung shut behind her. She answered with a grunt, and then she was gone, with a bang and rattle of wood. Eliza clenched her jaw and raced after her mother. "I'll be back soon," she called over her shoulder to Gabriel as she yanked open the door and stepped into the bright, cloudless day. "You can manage alone for a bit, *ya?*" Eliza didn't wait for an answer before the door slammed shut.

Eliza thudded across the narrow porch and down the wooden steps. The sunlight was too fierce, so she shielded her face with the blade of her hand as she crossed the gravel parking lot and followed Lovina across the farmyard, dodging chickens and mud puddles along the way.

"*Mamm*, wait," Eliza called out as she reached Lovina's side and tugged on her sleeve. "What are you going to say to Katie?"

"Nothing that you haven't already agreed to."

Eliza shook her head. "*Nee, Mamm.* You don't need to bring Katie into this. I told Gabriel I couldn't speak to him anymore." A surge of desperation shot through Eliza's body.

She could not bear to be humiliated on top of everything else.

"We both know that's impossible when you are working in that little shop together."

"He's going back to work on the farm soon. His ankle's almost healed."

"*Gut.* But until then I have to look out for you." Lovina bounded up the back-porch steps, faster than most women her age could manage. She made a beeline to the back door and pulled it open without knocking. "Katie?" she called out as she pushed her way into the spacious farmhouse kitchen. Katie stood at the sink, scrubbing a large saucepan. Mason jars filled with dark red beets lined the butcher block counter in neat, orderly rows.

"*Gude Mariye*, Lovina," Katie said without skipping a beat. She was used to Lovina making herself at home wherever she went. "What can I do for you today?"

"How do you know I didn't just *kumme* for a visit? It's been a while since we sat and chatted over *kaffi*."

Katie smiled faintly. "Did you just *kumme* for a visit?"

"*Nee*, but I *could* have."

Katie suppressed a chuckle and tucked a stray strand of auburn hair beneath her *kapp*.

"Well, I'm ready for a break, so I'll make *kaffi* anyway." She wrung soapy water out of her dishrag and spread it out beside the sink to dry.

"I know I'm supposed to be at the shop right now, but since Gabriel's there, do you mind if I stay?" Eliza gave Katie a nervous glance, and Katie frowned.

"Of course," Katie said. "Seems this might involve you, *ya*?"

Eliza gave a tight-lipped nod, adjusted her glasses and waited for the hammer to fall.

They took their coffee onto the wraparound porch and settled into the white rocking chairs that overlooked the farmyard. Chickens milled around the yard, pecking at the dirt and flapping their wings. Sunlight gleamed over the long rows of freshly planted soybeans that lay beyond the big red barn. Milk cows grazed in the damp, green south pasture. Levi drove a horse-powered tractor in a distant field, a trail of dust billowing behind him.

"I may as well come straight to the point," Lovina said as soon as she had taken her first sip of coffee.

"Never known you to do anything else," Katie said.

"The problem is with Gabriel," Lovina said. "He's not given us any trouble that I know of since he's been working in the shop," Katie said, her tone mild.

"Humph."

Eliza clutched her coffee mug tighter. She knew what was coming. "*Mamm*, there's really no need to—"

"He's tempted my Eliza."

Eliza gasped. "*Nee!* That isn't the way it is!"

Katie's attention jerked to Lovina. "That's a serious charge," she said, her tone no longer so mild. She looked from Lovina to Eliza.

"Nothing happened," Eliza said, her voice rising in pitch and tone. "We're just friends. We haven't done anything wrong."

Katie nodded and turned back to Lovina. "You heard Eliza."

Lovina's face tightened. "*Ya*, I did. And I also heard her last night when she admitted to falling in love with him."

Eliza could not believe her mother had just said those words out loud. She suddenly felt sick and set her coffee cup onto the side table, unable to stomach the sight or smell of it.

Katie sighed. "I figure that's between Eliza and Gabriel."

"Not when her future is at stake. You and I both know he's planning on jumping the fence. I won't let him take my *dochder* and *kinnskind* away with him. Don't you understand? Their souls are at stake!" A ripple of vulnerability briefly passed over Lovina's face before her expression hardened.

Katie hesitated, then asked quietly, "Is this true, Eliza? Is Gabriel planning to go *Englisch*?" She frowned and looked toward the little shop across the farmyard. Sunlight glinted off the windows, obscuring what was inside. "I know he has spoken of it in the past, but I thought he had worked through that and is trying to commit to our ways."

Eliza looked down at her hands in her lap. She unfolded and refolded them.

"Eliza?" Lovina asked sharply. "Answer her."

Eliza wanted to defend Gabriel, but she could not lie. She swallowed hard. "He told me this morning that he is planning on leaving. But—"

"There are no *but*s," Lovina interrupted. She sliced her hand through the air in a decisive motion. "This man is a danger to you, plain and simple. You just said it yourself."

"*Nee*, it's more complicated than that. He was upset—"

"That's no excuse. When you're upset, do you consider jumping the fence? Do you,

Katie? Do I? *Nee*, of course not. Only a bad heart jumps to bad intentions."

"We were just talking. And if I hadn't said—"

"Enough, Eliza." Lovina shook her head. "This isn't about anything you've said. That boy has had his heart set on leaving for years. He still isn't baptized, ain't so? He's been dragging his feet for years. He's got one foot in the *Englisch* world already."

Eliza wanted to argue, but everything her mother said was true, strictly speaking. She knew the situation was more nuanced than Lovina presented it as being, but Eliza couldn't argue with the facts. Gabriel wasn't baptized. He had not ended his *rumspringa*. Eliza, on the other hand, had never even indulged in one. Maybe her mother was right. Her heart shouted otherwise, but what did the heart know? Lovina had laid out the truth, clear and simple. And Gabriel himself had announced he was leaving. Eliza buried her face in her hands.

"I can see you are both very upset about this," Katie said. Eliza noticed she wasn't taking sides, but she wasn't defending Gabriel anymore either.

"You better believe I am," Lovina said.

"Please don't say anything," Eliza whispered.

"What?" Lovina asked. "We can't hear you."

Eliza dropped her hands from her face, but kept her gaze down. "Please don't say anything to Gabriel. He doesn't know…" She hesitated, then added in a small voice, "…that I'm in love with him." Eliza risked a quick glance at Katie. Her face looked sympathetic but serious. Eliza wanted to sink into the floor and disappear. She had kept her love hidden for years. She couldn't bear for Gabriel—and the rest of Bluebird Hills—to learn her deepest, most embarrassing secret.

Katie put a hand on Eliza's arm and squeezed. "No one needs to know." She dropped her hand and cut Lovina a look. "They won't hear it from me."

Lovina huffed and looked away.

Eliza felt as if she were slowly sinking. How had everything gone so wrong, so quickly?

"So what exactly do you want me to do, Lovina?" Katie asked. "I assume you're not here just to tell me the facts."

Lovina gave a quick nod and straightened up in her seat. "Eliza must stop working at the gift shop until Gabriel stops working there."

Katie let out a small, almost-imperceptible sigh. "If you really insist…"

"I do," Lovina said.

"*Oll recht.* Eliza can take a leave of absence until then. I don't think it will be very long from now. His ankle is healing nicely, I hear."

"But don't you need me?" Eliza glanced from Katie to her mother with pleading eyes.

"I do. And I'd rather you stay. But I can see that this is going to cause trouble I'd rather avoid."

Eliza stiffened. "I don't cause trouble." Hadn't she always stuck to the rules?

"*Nee*, you don't," Katie replied.

Lovina pursed her lips at the implication.

Eliza gripped her hands together in her lap. They felt sweaty and hot. "I don't want to leave you without the help you need."

"It's *oll recht.* I'll manage. Gabriel can cover in the shop when I can't be there. He's learned a lot since you've been teaching him the ropes."

"And you won't tell him why I'm leaving?" Eliza pushed her glasses up the bridge of her nose and stared at Katie. "You promise?"

Katie crossed, then uncrossed her legs. "I promise," she said after a moment's hesitation. "Though I fear that will cause more problems down the road."

"*Nee.* This is for the best. *Danki.*" Eliza gripped her hands together. She could feel hot tears of relief pricking at her eyes. "*Danki* so much for keeping my secret."

Katie nodded, but her expression looked troubled.

Gabriel waited for Eliza to return from the farmhouse. She never did. An hour passed, then two. He finally left the shop to check around back and saw that her buggy was gone. He had heard the clatter of hoofbeats and the grind of buggy wheels earlier but thought that had been Lovina leaving. He had not realized that Eliza was following her.

He frowned as he tapped a pen against the countertop. Minding the shop was boring without Eliza. He tapped the pen harder. Did she leave because of him? Had he been too hard on her? She did have a point, after all. His heart had been set on leaving for a long time…

Gabriel shot up from his chair, which was not easy to do. He knocked over one of his crutches and nearly lost his balance as he fumbled not to put too much weight on his ankle. He braced a hand against the countertop, leaned down and picked up his crutch, then gingerly tested how much his ankle could take.

He was surprised to find it could manage

more weight than he had realized. He could probably put away the crutches in another day or two. This was good news because the faster he healed, the faster he could get out of the shop and away from all the memories of Eliza.

For now, his ankle was well enough to pace, which he was itching to do. He began to hobble along the worn floorboards, the wood creaking beneath each slow, deliberate step. Thoughts whipped through his head as he moved. Had he driven Eliza away, or had she been the one at fault? He replayed the conversation in his mind, the best he could remember it. But each time he did, the words got a little hazier and the guilt got a little heavier.

If he were a better man, his relationship with Eliza would look a lot different right now. She wanted—*deserved*—a man who would commit to her and to the faith. Sure, he had been ready to do that, but that commitment had come too late. He had lived too wild for too long, and now he had to pay the price. How could he have ever expected an upright woman like Eliza to give him a chance?

She was too smart for that.

Gabriel reached the end of the aisle, turned and started back again. He didn't stop until the door swung open and Katie strode in. She flashed a confident smile, but he detected unease behind it.

"You're up and walking?" she asked.

"*Ya*. Trying, anyway." His ankle was throbbing, but he had been so agitated and distracted he hadn't noticed until now.

"*Gut* to see you're on the mend."

Gabriel nodded and headed back toward his chair behind the counter. *"Danki."* He sank into his seat and studied Katie as she realigned a row of bushel baskets filled with sugar peas, radishes and spring onions. Her mouth was too tight around the edges. "How are you doing?" Gabriel asked.

"Fine."

Gabriel raised his eyebrows. "Really?"

Katie hesitated. "*Ach*, it's nothing much. Just that Eliza has to take a short leave of absence from the shop."

Gabriel's stomach plummeted. Eliza refused to work with him now? It was one thing to leave for the day, but this was a whole other level.

She *really* didn't want anything to do with him.

Katie gave Gabriel a reassuring smile. "Don't look so worried. We'll manage *oll recht*. You've been doing a *gut* job."

Gabriel ignored the comment and cut right to the point. "Did she say why she's leaving? And how soon she'll be back?"

Katie cleared her throat and turned her attention to a bushel basket of spring onions. She slid the basket back a quarter inch to line up with the others. "Oh, I don't know when she'll be back exactly…" She brushed a sprinkle of dirt from a handwritten label on the wooden shelf beneath the baskets. "It depends on how…things work out."

Was Eliza waiting to return until after he went back to doing farmwork? Why else would Katie be so evasive? Gabriel narrowed his eyes. "You haven't said why she's leaving. They need the money, ain't so? Must be something serious." A clang of panic zipped through him. "It isn't Priss, is it?" He had not thought of that until now.

"Nee." Katie shook her head. *"Nee,* nothing like that. No need to worry."

If she knew that he didn't need to worry, then she knew what was wrong. She just wasn't telling him. He planted his forearms on the counter and leaned forward. "It's me, isn't it?"

Katie made a little noise of surprise. A spring onion slipped from her fingers; then she caught it. She set it down gently in a basket and turned around to face him. "Why would you ask a thing like that, Gabriel?"

Gabriel raised an eyebrow. "You're being mighty indirect. A lack of denial is as good as a confirmation." Gabriel knew that Katie might change the subject to distract him, but she would never lie. It wasn't in her nature.

Katie stared at him. She opened her mouth, then closed it again.

"Well?" Gabriel asked.

"Eliza's business is her own. It isn't my place to say."

"You've already said enough," Gabriel mumbled.

"What?"

"It doesn't matter. I know all I need to know."

Katie shook her head. It looked like she was about to say something. Indecision flickered across her features; then she sighed and turned back to the shelves. "She'll be back soon," she murmured.

But Gabriel wasn't listening anymore. He was too busy thinking about the lengths Eliza was willing to go to in order to avoid him.

Chapter Twelve

Eliza didn't know what to do with herself. Her fingers itched to punch the keys on the cash register or rearrange the display shelves at Aunt Fannie's Amish Gift Shop. Instead, she was stuck at home. She felt purposeless and unproductive without having a till to balance at the end of the day. The sense of satisfaction after a good day of sales had always meant so much to her.

Worst of all, she kept replaying her last conversation with Gabriel. She couldn't believe she had said the things she had. He deserved better. But she had to honor her mother.

Being caught between the two people she loved felt like a knife twisting in her gut.

Eliza decided the best thing to do was to stay busy, so she organized the pantry, then deep-cleaned the kitchen. By the time Priss came home from school, the room sparkled and shone, and the scent of pine-scented cleaning solution wafted in the air. "You're home early!" Priss dropped her lunch pail and launched herself into Eliza's arms as the pail clattered across the floor.

Lovina appeared in the doorway. "What's all the racket? I can hear it from the yard."

"Priss is surprised to see me," Eliza said as she buried her face in the girl's hair. She smelled like sunshine and grass.

"Here," Priss said as she pulled away from Eliza's arms and yanked a yellow wildflower from her pocket. "I picked it at recess for you."

Eliza took the wilted, crumpled flower and smiled. "It's perfect."

Priss beamed. "I knew you'd like it."

"I've got to unhitch Bunny," Lovina said and turned back toward the doorway. "Just came to see what the commotion was."

"Why are you home early, *Mamm*?" Priss asked Eliza.

Lovina paused in the threshold.

"Can we go see the llamas behind the Yoder farm since you're home?" Priss added before Eliza could answer her first question. "Gabriel said we could go sometime. Can we all go now?"

Lovina stiffened, then turned around. She gave Eliza a level stare as they waited for an answer.

Eliza cleared her throat and looked down at the flower in her hand. "*Ach*, well…" She smoothed out the soft stem with a thumb and finger. "Not today."

"But why?" Priss tugged on Eliza's apron. "He promised we'd go."

"Not everyone keeps their promises," Lovina said from the doorway.

Priss looked confused.

Eliza frowned and shook her head at her mother. "I'm sure that doesn't apply to Gabriel."

Lovina raised an eyebrow but didn't contradict her out loud.

"So we can go?" Priss bounced onto her tiptoes with excitement.

"*Nee*. Gabriel has to work at the shop, especially now that I'm not there."

"After work?" She cut her eyes to the battery-powered clock on the kitchen wall. "I can wait until then."

Lovina watched as Eliza searched for a response. "Um, not today."

"Tomorrow?"

"*Nee*, not tomorrow."

Priss planted her fists on her hips. "Then when?"

Eliza turned away, walked to the kitchen cabinets and pulled out a plastic blue vase.

"When?" Priss repeated.

Eliza didn't answer. Instead, she turned on the tap and filled the vase with water.

"*Mamm*, you're not answering me!"

Eliza sighed and flicked off the tap. "I tell you what. Why don't we go right now? Then you don't have to wait."

Priss shook her head, hands still on her hips. "*Nee*. I want to wait for Gabriel. It will be more fun that way. He's always fun. And he'll make the llamas less scary. He told me he'll stand between me and the one that spits so it will get him instead of me."

Eliza's heart ached. "I can do that instead."

"*Nee*. You're too small. It'll spit right over your head and onto me."

Eliza laughed, even though she felt like crying. "You might be right about that."

"Gabriel made up a song about llamas the other day. It rhymed and everything, and it was so funny that Simon spit out his milk when he heard it. I wish I could remember it. If I could,

I would tell it to you. Have you ever spit out your milk before?"

Lovina held up a hand. She was still hovering in the doorway, watching the interaction. "We do not need to hear the song. Sounds like he's playing with fire, making up secular lyrics like that. The *Ausbund* provides all the music we need."

Eliza let out a sharp sigh before she could stop herself. "I'm sure it was just a harmless game to entertain the *kinner, Mamm.*"

"Plenty of things start out harmless enough. Haven't you heard that the road to wickedness is paved with good intentions?"

"*Ya.* From you," Eliza gave her mother a level stare. "All the time."

"*Gut,* then we're agreed."

They were most certainly *not* in agreement, but Eliza knew it was pointless to argue with her mother. She dropped the yellow wildflower into the vase and set it on the windowsill above the sink. Afternoon sunlight filtered in through the freshly scrubbed windowpanes and sparkled against the water.

"Right, Eliza? You *do* agree, *ya*?"

Eliza adjusted the vase's position on the windowsill to avoid her mother's eyes.

Lovina clucked her tongue. "You've changed,

Eliza. And that just proves that I'm right about Gab—"

"Shh!" Eliza spun around and pressed a finger to her lips. "That's enough. I understand, *oll recht*?" She felt a sudden fierce need to defend Gabriel. It was bad enough to cut him out of Priss's life. She would not let him be defamed in the girl's eyes as well.

Lovina shook her head. "I'm disappointed in you, Eliza."

Eliza's instinct was to look down, nod in agreement and promise to do better. But she could not. Something imperceptible had shifted within her these last weeks. Lovina was right— she *was* different. "Haven't I done enough?" Eliza asked in a low, hard voice. "I did what you asked. Can't you let it go now?"

Lovina narrowed her eyes. She opened her mouth to speak, then shook her head, turned around and thundered down the back steps. "Horse needs tending to," she said over her shoulder. "Can't stand around yapping."

Eliza snorted as she watched her mother flee the conversation. It felt good to stand up to herself. She could get used to that kind of satisfaction.

But what if her mother was right? It was true that Eliza had been as meek as a kitten before she got to know Gabriel. And now, she just couldn't keep her mouth shut. Oh sure, she had been outspoken at times but not to her mother. And never about bending the rules— only about keeping them.

In short, she had been just like Lovina.

And now she wasn't.

The realization slapped Eliza like a wave of cold water. Had she finally managed to climb out of her mother's shadow?

"Mamm?"

Eliza's attention jerked to Priss, who was staring at her with a crumpled expression. "What is it, sweetheart?"

"What did Gabriel do wrong?"

"Nothing," she said without thinking. "Nothing at all."

"Then why can't I see him?"

Eliza didn't have an answer.

Gabriel had not heard from his father in a very long time. He figured no news was good news. The only time his father ever contacted him was to remind him that he ought to come home, do his duty and live up to expectations. So Gabriel's stomach tightened when he arrived home that evening and Mary met him at the front door with a letter in her hand.

"This can't be *gut*," he murmured as he studied the return address. His father's handwriting was perfect, each line straight and bold, each letter precisely formed. Just seeing those words sent a jolt through him as he remembered how his father used to hit him on the hand with a ruler for having messy handwriting. No matter how hard Gabriel had tried, he simply couldn't get the letters to look as neat as his father's.

"Gabriel? Are you *oll recht*?"

"Huh?" His eyes jerked from the letter to Mary.

"I asked if you're *oll recht*."

Gabriel swallowed and forced what he hoped looked like a carefree smile. "*Ach*, just thinking. You know me—never paying attention."

Mary didn't look convinced. "I know it's hard to get these letters." She bit her lip and looked down at the envelope in his hand. "Maybe I should open it for you. I could read it first…soften the blow." She reached for the letter. "In fact, it's probably best if you never read it at all. Maybe you don't even need to know what it says."

Gabriel pulled his hand back before she could take the envelope. "*Nee*. He's my *daed*. I'll deal with it."

"*Ya*, but he's my *bruder*. I know how he

treats people. It isn't right. And treating his own *sohn* the way he has…" She let the words die away and shook her head.

Gabriel sighed. "I'm sure it's just more of the same. It won't make anything worse than it already is."

"At least let me get you some tea. I put the kettle on already. Thought it might help a little."

"Ya." He wanted to tell her he didn't need any support. It was just a letter, after all. But just thinking about his father made his stomach twist into knots. Reading a letter from him was sure to make him feel even worse.

"Gut." Mary patted him on the shoulder. "You go sit down in the living room. I'll be right there."

Gabriel went over to the old upholstered chair, propped his crutches against the nearby wall, pushed an embroidered pillow aside and sank into the seat. Gray clouds hung low in the sky outside the window, leaving the room cool and dim. He could hear the clang of metal through the walls, then the familiar tread of Mary's steady footsteps. She appeared in the doorway, holding a tray of oatmeal cookies and two mugs. Good-smelling steam rose upward, filling the room with a quiet comfort. "Mmm," Gabriel murmured. "Mint. My favorite."

"I know." Mary smiled, set the tray in front of him and settled into one of the wooden gliders. She did not pick up her mug or her plate of cookies.

Gabriel stared at the envelope in his hands. He let out a big exhalation, then ripped open the top of the envelope. He pulled out the letter and unfolded it.

"Here," Mary said and pushed a mug of hot tea into his free hand. He nodded and blew across the top as his eyes skimmed the first few lines of the letter. The words *disappointed, disloyal, failure* and *embarrassment* stood out to him.

"What does it say?" Mary asked. She leaned forward in her seat slightly.

"Just more of the same," Gabriel said. Then he saw something that made his stomach drop to his toes. "*Nee,* wait…"

Mary leaned in closer. Her fingers tightened in her lap. "What is it?"

Gabriel reread the paragraph to himself. He needed time for it to sink in. He could hear the quiet rasp of Mary's breath, the distant clatter of hooves and buggy wheels over pavement, the gentle whisper of wind rustling the oak leaves outside the window.

"Gabriel?" Mary asked after a long stretch of silence.

Gabriel set his mug on the coffee table without taking a sip, then crumpled the paper in his fist and threw it across the room. Mary watched with concerned eyes.

"He's giving the farm to cousin Abner instead of me."

"But Abner doesn't need the farm! He has a *gut* farm of his own. And he's such a distant relative that he's barely family. What is he—a fifth or sixth cousin, or something like that?"

"Something like that," Gabriel muttered. "Three or four times removed or…" He shook his head. "It doesn't matter."

Mary's jaw tightened. "It does matter. It matters very much."

Gabriel let out a bitter laugh. "Tell that to *Daed*, then."

Mary didn't have an answer to that. They both knew he would not listen to her—or anyone, for that matter, except maybe the bishop. But why would the bishop in his father's church district intervene?

"What about his bishop?" Mary asked. "He might see reason."

"You know as well as I do that *Daed* has always told everyone how wayward I am," Gabriel said. "He's said it so many times that no one questions it anymore." Gabriel shook his head. "And why should they? I've given them just enough evidence to make *Daed's* opinion of me believable."

"You're not a bad man, Gabriel."

"*Nee*, but I haven't been baptized. I own a laptop and a cell phone. I've been tempted to jump the fence for a long time, and everyone knows that."

"You just need support," Mary said quietly. "That's all. And if your *daed* gave it to you, you wouldn't feel the need to go to the *Englisch* for it."

Gabriel stared at the crumbled ball of paper across the room. "Maybe. But no one cares why I do what I do. They only care that I do it."

They sat without speaking for a moment, then Mary asked, "Why now? What's happened that he's giving away the farm?"

"He says he's getting old and wants to move into the *dawdihaus* and take it easy. He says Abner will take care of him and deserves the farm in exchange for his loyalty. When *Daed* dies, Abner gets everything."

"Maybe there's still time to change his mind," Mary said. "That farm is your rightful inheritance. You could make a *gut*, honest home there—find a *gut* wife, settle down…"

"*Nee*, it's too late for that. He wrote to tell me that he already changed his will. It's done. And you know once something is done, *Daed* doesn't change his mind."

Mary's eyes welled with tears that she quickly wiped with the hem of her sleeve. "I thought that farm would keep you here. It would have given you a sense of place, a reason to make a commitment." Mary shook her head. "I'm so afraid for you, Gabriel. It feels like your life is hanging by a thread, and your *daed* just snapped that thread."

Gabriel picked up the mug of mint tea. He held it in his hands but didn't drink it. He just wanted to feel the warmth. "That thread snapped a long time ago."

"*Nee!* Don't say that."

Gabriel thought of Eliza and how he had almost asked her to walk out with him. For the first time, he had imagined a life here, in Bluebird Hills, living as the Amish man everyone wanted him to be. But Eliza saw him the same way his father did: a troublemaker. "There's nothing left to keep me here, *Aenti* Mary."

"But…" Mary shook her head hard. "You have me."

Gabriel's expression softened. He reached out and put a hand on hers. "I know. And that means the world to me. But I need a life—my own life. I can't live in your house forever. I've got to make my own way." He lifted his hand from hers.

Mary nodded. "I understand. But can't you make your own way here in Bluebird Hills, where you belong? What do you think you'll find out there amongst strangers? Do you really think they will care for you more than us, your own people?" Mary's voice was calm, but her eyes looked desperate. "And what about *Gott*? Will you turn your back on Him?"

Gabriel felt his heart tearing as he watched her pain. *"Nee,"* he answered quietly, his gaze steady.

"But if you leave…"

"Maybe *Gott* is bigger than we think."

"Don't make up fancy philosophical explanations to excuse what you're doing."

Gabriel sighed and looked away. "I have to leave." He didn't know why, exactly. He just knew he couldn't stay where he wasn't wanted or understood. He wasn't sure what he would find in the *Englisch* world, but he hoped it was acceptance. And he hoped God would be there, too, just like He was in Bluebird Hills.

"I wish it wasn't all so tangled up together."

"What do you mean?"

"You, *Gott*, being Amish, Eliza—" He clamped his mouth shut as soon as he realized what he had said.

Mary narrowed her eyes. "Eliza Zook? What's she got to do with all this?"

"Nothing. I can't stay here, where I'm not wanted, so all I can do is hope that I can find *Gott* outside of the *Ordnung*."

Mary looked at Gabriel like she wanted to say a thousand things to him, but she kept her composure and only spoke one sentence: "God can find us anywhere, Gabriel, but you'll never see that if your back is turned."

Chapter Thirteen

Gabriel's mind was made up. There was nothing keeping him in Bluebird Hills any longer. He spent a long, lonely day in the shop, then headed straight home, full of determination. After stabling Comet, he stormed through the front door of the house, headed to the stairs and then stopped. He set his crutches against the wall and gingerly placed his bad foot on the bottom step. No pain. Or not too much, anyway. He was well enough to get on with life.

It was time to go.

He spent the next twenty minutes packing. That was all the time it took to fit a Plain life into a suitcase. He took his three work shirts and his good-for-church shirt from the hook on his bedroom wall, folded them and put them in his suitcase. Then he added his three pairs of dark pants, his spare pair of suspenders, his heavy coat, and his black felt hat for Sundays and cold-weather days. After that, the hooks on the wall were bare.

Gabriel added his small collection of dog-eared paperbacks and snorted when he tossed them into the suitcase. No need to keep them a secret anymore. He packed his wood carving kit that he used to make Amish knick-knacks to sell to tourists at the gift shop. He would tell Mary to take whatever consignment money Katie owed him for any carvings that sold after he left. He had a small display shelf in the shop that sold out pretty regularly. He probably wouldn't have any place to sell his carvings after this—he couldn't expect Katie to do business with him after he went *Englisch*—but he could still carve for pleasure. It always calmed him to whittle a block of wood beside the flickering light of the woodstove, especially on cold winter nights when darkness drove him inside for the evening.

Of course, he would probably get a television now. Wasn't that what *Englischers* did? He stared at the wood carving kit in his suitcase, debated for a moment and left it there. Maybe it would comfort him to have something to do with his hands that reminded him of home, even though he would have fancy entertainment to keep him occupied.

The thought of sitting alone in an apartment under the harsh glare of electric lights, watching television, sent a jolt of panic through him. Was that what he really wanted? What did he honestly think he would find alone among the *Englisch*?

Gabriel frowned as his eyes moved to the Bible on his bedside table. The last item to pack. Would *Gott* still be with him as he read His book by the light of an electric lamp? Should he even bother to bring it? Would *Gott* listen to his prayers if they were whispered above the din of traffic or the whirr of an air-conditioning unit?

Gabriel grabbed the big leather-bound Bible and placed it carefully on top of the stack of shirts. He knew he couldn't leave it behind. There was so much of Bluebird Hills he wanted to take with him. His heart felt so full of ache and confusion that he slumped onto the bed, put his face in his hands and questioned why he was leaving at all.

Maybe it was worth giving Bluebird Hills one more chance. All he wanted was to be accepted. He could go to Eliza... Gabriel dropped his hands and straightened up. Yes, that was it. He would go to Eliza. He would tell her that he was leaving and see what she said. If she tried to stop him, then he would stay. He would know that at least one person other than Aunt Mary thought he was worthy of being Amish.

He would leave it in Eliza's hands.

Gabriel gave a grim nod to himself, stood up and headed out the door. He was on a mission. And the result would determine the course of his entire life.

Gabriel had never hitched up a buggy horse so quickly. His fingers fumbled over the buckles and straps, the metal jangling and leather creaking as he worked. Comet whinnied and craned her neck to watch him as he tugged at a buckle, his mouth set in a taut line. She stomped a hoof and stared at him.

"Guess you can tell I'm a little worked up, ain't so?" Gabriel patted her flank, then reached for the next buckle. She pushed her nose into his face until he patted her again. Gabriel felt a pang of loneliness even though he hadn't left Bluebird Hills yet. This could be the last time he felt the velvety-soft caress of Comet's muzzle, heard the clink of the harness, smelled the earthy scent of horse. "I haven't really thought about how much I'm going to miss you," Gabriel said. He scratched under Comet's chin until she snorted and swung her head away, no longer interested. "I can't take you with me. But Mary will take *gut* care of you." He almost said *until I return*, but this decision was permanent. He would not return, even though that concept felt unreal. Lancaster County, Pennsylvania and the Amish faith were all he had ever known. Was it really possible to walk away forever?

Perhaps he wouldn't have to. But that depended on Eliza. He set his face in a determined expression, gave Comet a final pat and climbed into the buggy. He would find out soon enough.

The drive felt like it took forever. Cars piled up behind him, waited for a chance to pass and then darted into the opposite lane to roar past him. Comet trotted on, hooves clip-clopping against pavement in a steady beat, undeterred. She was used to the din of traffic and the rush of hot wind as trucks rumbled past them. She knew to stay on course, slow and steady. That was the Amish way.

But Gabriel wished he were in one of the vehicles speeding past the rolling hills and yellow cornfields. Then he would be at Eliza's in no time. Slow and steady had never felt right to him. He liked to keep moving, his attention always darting to the next event on the horizon. He never had been able to sit still, and his father used to shout at Gabriel when he fidgeted in his chair. Then his father would follow up his admonishment with a stinging slap on the leg to make sure Gabriel got the message. Just another reminder that Gabriel was not cut out to be Amish.

Finally, the road narrowed and traffic slowed as Gabriel neared Bluebird Hills' downtown. They trotted along Main Street, past the quaint row of mom-and-pop shops with handwritten signs lined up beneath the old oak trees that shaded the sidewalk. He remembered all the times he had popped into the bakery for a fresh-baked cinnamon roll, browsed the bookstore or stopped by the hardware store to pick up a few supplies for the Miller farm. Today the owner's brindle bulldog was lounging in the open doorway, as he always did, watching the traffic go by.

Gabriel tried not to think about how much he would miss those simple, everyday memories: the smell of leather and paper in the bookstore, the creak of the worn wooden floorboards in the hardware store, and the way the owner's dog always jumped up to greet him.

Gabriel refused to look anymore. He kept his eyes straight ahead, clenched his jaw and flicked the reins to hurry Comet along. Soon, they passed the last shop, and houses with tidy yards and white picket fences appeared alongside the road. Some houses had electric porch lights and cars in the driveway. Others had the telltale green shades in the windows that marked them as Lancaster County Amish. None of the homes, *Englisch* or Amish, were like the farmhouses outside of town that had rambling porches, weathered outbuildings and yards worn bare from livestock. These homes were neat, orderly and predictable, just like Eliza. It was only right she lived here.

Her redbrick ranch came into view, and Gabriel steered his horse into the driveway. His palms felt damp against the leather reins. He patted the sweat from his forehead with his shirtsleeve, then wiped it from his hands, took a deep breath and clambered down from the buggy. He secured Comet to a hitching post alongside the driveway and bounded toward the front door. His ankle sent a sharp reminder to take it easy, but he ignored the warning.

He needed to talk to Eliza. Now.

He had almost made it to the front door

when it swung open and Lovina hurried outside, wiping her hands on her apron. "You! What do you want?" she asked.

Gabriel stopped short. He glanced at the house, then back to Lovina. "I want to speak to Eliza."

Lovina's face tightened. "She doesn't want to talk to you."

He frowned. "It's important. Tell her it's urgent."

"*Nee*, I can't do that. She said she won't be talking to you anymore."

Gabriel froze, unsure how to react. His heartbeat thudded in his ears. "Are you sure? Just go ask her. Please."

"I don't need to. We've already discussed it. She won't talk to you. And that's final."

"But I'm leaving. This is the last chance—"

"I knew it!" Lovina said, cutting him off. "This is exactly why she won't speak to you. She knows the way you are."

Gabriel stared at Lovina as his stomach sank to the ground.

"And now you've proven it by leaving." Lovina pointed her finger at him. "Don't *kumme* back here, Gabriel. We don't want anything to do with your ways."

Gabriel felt pulled between anger, disbelief

and grief. He wanted so badly to rush past Lovina, push his way inside the house and shout for Eliza. He wanted to tell her he didn't want to leave but that he couldn't stay unless he knew she was with him. He couldn't be alone in a tight-knit community anymore. He couldn't be an outsider while living on the inside. He needed her to stand with him.

"Please," he managed to say in a shaky voice. "I need to speak with her."

Lovina hesitated and Gabriel thought she was going to soften her stance; but instead, she shook her head as a pained expression clouded her face. "If you truly care about her, then you will leave her alone. You won't tempt her. You will respect her wishes. She deserves to live an upright life with an upright man. She deserves to find peace and security."

Gabriel felt a wave of regret and self-loathing sweep over him. Lovina was right. Eliza deserved better. He should never have come.

"Please," Lovina added, her voice dropping to a pleading whisper. "Please don't *kumme* back."

Gabriel stood frozen for a terrible moment, then spun around on his heels and stumbled back to the buggy.

He knew what he had to do.

* * *

Eliza was mopping her bedroom when she heard a knock on the door. She had spent the day scrubbing the house from top to bottom in order to get her mind off Gabriel. She straightened up, stretched her back and sighed. Gabriel was still heavy on her mind, no matter how much she tried to distract herself. She heard the front door open down the hall, then the murmur of voices through the walls. Eliza wondered who would come by in the middle of the day, when most people were busy working.

A jolt of excitement pulsed through her at the thought that it might be Gabriel. But the emotion disintegrated as quickly as it had come. Even if he did show up, she would have to send him away—if her mother didn't first, which she probably would.

Eliza heard footsteps moving across the house, then the creak of the sofa as someone sat down in the living room. She untied her soiled work apron and quickly replaced it with one fresh from the clothesline, crisply starched and smelling of sunshine. She reminded herself that Gabriel could not possibly be in her living room, but her feet hurried from the bedroom and down the hall all the same, her heart skipping a beat as she rounded the corner to the living room.

Katie sat on the sofa, her brows knitted together in concern. Eliza's stomach dropped as she stumbled to a halt. Something was wrong. It was written all over Katie's face. "It's Gabriel, isn't it?" Eliza whispered. "Why else would you leave the shop at this time of day? You're not here for a social call, that's for certain sure."

"*Nee*, I'm not here for a social call. I had to leave Levi in charge to get away."

"So Gabriel isn't there…"

Katie shook her head and looked away.

Lovina rushed into the living room with a tray of iced tea and lemon cookies. "What's happened?" she asked. "Have you told her anything yet?"

"*Nee,*" Katie said.

"Told me what?" Eliza asked, her attention darting from Katie to her mother, then back again.

Lovina set a glass of iced tea and a plate of cookies in front of Katie. *"Danki,"* Katie murmured, but she made no move toward the refreshments.

Eliza stepped closer. She could sense the heaviness in the room. Everyone but her knew that something terrible had happened—something they didn't want to tell her. "Has there been another accident?" She gripped the back of one of the gliders for support. "Is Gabriel *oll recht*?"

"Why don't you sit down?" Katie asked.

"Why don't you tell me what's happened?"

Katie gave a quick nod and drew a deep breath. "Gabriel has left, Eliza."

Eliza's hand tightened around the wooden slats of the glider. "What do you mean, left?"

"He jumped the fence this morning."

"You mean he…" Eliza eased around to the front of the glider, then sat down hard.

Katie leaned over and put a reassuring hand on Eliza's knee. "*Ya.* I'm afraid so."

Tears welled in Eliza's eyes before she could force them back. "But he didn't say goodbye."

Lovina cleared her throat and pushed the tray of cookies toward Eliza. "Here, try to eat something."

Eliza turned her head.

Lovina sighed through her nose and set the tray on the coffee table with a hard thump. "I know it hurts now, but it's for the best. I hope you can see that."

A tremor formed deep inside Eliza, then slowly grew until her body began to shake.

"For the best?" Eliza was not sure what she was feeling. "For the best?" Eliza repeated, louder this time. Her eyes swung to her mother. And then she realized what the unfamiliar feeling was: anger. She had spent so long being perfect that she had not allowed herself to feel this before. And now it was pouring out of her physically. She clasped her hands together to stop the shaking but could still feel the sensation rippling through the rest of her body. "How dare you say that this is for the best? Gabriel is lost now. We all rejected him, and now he's turned away from the faith."

"Now, Eliza. I know how you felt about him—"

"How I *felt*? I still love him. I'll always love him. Just because he's gone from the faith doesn't mean he's gone from my heart."

Lovina looked away.

"I'm sorry, Eliza," Katie said quietly. "I feel partially responsible. I keep thinking, if only I had said something, tried harder…" She held up her hands. "I don't know…"

"We're all to blame," Eliza said. "*All* of us. No one made him feel accepted. We all let him go on believing that his father was right."

Katie inhaled sharply.

"It isn't that simple," Lovina said. "Gabriel is a grown man. He made his own decision."

"A decision that his father and the community drove him toward his entire life."

"Perhaps there's a reason for that," Lovina said.

Eliza's breath caught in her throat. "I can't believe you just said that." This could not be happening. Gabriel could not have left. Eliza wanted to wake up and learn it was all a bad dream. No one spoke for a moment. Eliza exhaled and tried to collect herself. "I blame myself more than anyone else."

Katie shook her head. "*Nee*, Eliza. Please don't do that to yourself."

"I told him I couldn't speak to him anymore. I let him feel like he was a bad influence, a bad man."

"You did what you had to do to protect Priss," Lovina said. "And don't you see? His actions have proved you right! He was going to leave no matter what you did. He's been planning this for years. Everyone knows that. We didn't push him away. We just recognized what was in him."

Katie shifted in her seat. "I… I wouldn't put it like that, exactly." She frowned and picked at a wrinkle on the skirt of her dress. "But Lovina's right when she says his mind was made up before the two of you got close."

Lovina nodded.

"It wasn't anything you said, Eliza. Levi's been worried about Gabriel for years. It's why he kept him on even though his heart wasn't always in the job. It was clear his attention was on the *Englisch world*, but Levi hoped to be a *gut* influence, to show Gabriel that there were people in Bluebird Hills who cared about him and believed in him..." Katie's voice trailed away, and she shook her head. "But I guess we couldn't reach him in the end."

"Still, if only I had said more, done more—" Eliza's voice cracked, and she couldn't finish the sentence.

"*Nee*, you can't blame yourself." Katie leaned forward and gave Eliza's arm a reassuring squeeze. "Believe me, it's my instinct too. But Gabriel is responsible for his own decisions. We can't blame ourselves for another's actions."

"I wish it were that simple."

"I think that sometimes we blame ourselves because it's too hard to blame the other person. Strangely enough, that can hurt even more."

Eliza frowned. She adjusted her glasses and thought about what Katie had said. Gabriel had not said goodbye to her. If he cared about her or about the faith, wouldn't he have made more effort? Wouldn't he have come to talk to her before leaving? Maybe he did hold more blame for this than she was willing to admit.

She felt the anger coursing through her shift toward him. "I don't know. I'm so confused." Eliza rocked the glider as she contemplated, her eyes on her lap. "He didn't say goodbye." A tear formed in her eye, and she wiped it away in a careless gesture. "He didn't even try to talk about it. I would have stopped him. I would have done *something*, if only he had cared enough to let me."

Lovina cleared her throat and stood up abruptly. "*Ach*, look at the time. I best put dinner on. We have a roast planned, and it needs to go in now to be ready on time."

"Oh." Katie looked from Lovina to Eliza. "I, uh, don't want to overstay. You probably need time to process this. But if there's anything I can do, you'll let me know, *ya*?" Katie's expression looked sincere and full of pain. "I wish things hadn't ended this way."

"Me too," Eliza murmured. She kept rocking and moved her eyes to the window, where a cardinal pecked at the bird feeder in the front yard. Katie sat beside her for a moment before rising to her feet and quietly slipping away. Eliza said nothing as Katie's footsteps echoed through the living room and down the hallway, and the front door opened and thudded shut.

She had a lot to think about.

Chapter Fourteen

Gabriel found a cheap studio apartment over-looking a shopping center. He had a handful of *Englisch* acquaintances whom he thought would help him get settled in, but he soon realized they had only come over to share a beer. He wasn't interested and shook his head at the offer. They left soon after, and Gabriel sat alone in his dingy one-room apartment, staring through the grimy window at the big-box store across the parking lot.

Gabriel's stomach sank when he realized he was just as alone here, in the bustling city of Lancaster, as he had been in Bluebird Hills. Somehow, he had expected to feel different once he cut ties and walked out. But he was still the same old Gabriel. He looked at his hands. They had the same calluses from farmwork; the same long, broad fingers; the same scar from where a tractor blade had cut him a year ago. They would be the same hands whether they held the reins to a horse-drawn cultivator or gripped a steering wheel and flipped on electric-light switches.

Traffic pulled in and out of the huge parking lot, horns beeped and strangers hurried in and out of the generic-looking storefronts. He already missed the wet, green grass and familiar faces of Bluebird Hills.

The problem was, those faces didn't miss him.

Gabriel managed to find a job washing dishes in a restaurant at the far end of the shopping center. He needed to stay within walking distance to his apartment because he couldn't afford to buy a car. He could take the bus, but it felt overwhelming to pack in between strangers who pretended he didn't exist even while they had to sit crammed against him.

Gabriel had hoped to make friends at work, but he only got a few polite nods. Mostly he got strange looks. Even though he had gone to the big-box store and bought new clothes, he knew he didn't quite look the part. He felt like he was playing dress-up and everyone could see it, especially when he opened his mouth to speak and his Pennsylvania Dutch accent gave him away. The only conversation anyone at work wanted to have with him was why he had left the Amish. He wanted to tell them there was more to him than his Amish background, but they couldn't seem to understand that.

The strangest thing was, he kept finding himself defending the Amish faith. Finally, one of his coworkers turned away from the vat of dishes he was spraying with hot water, shook his head and said, "Why'd you leave if it's so great?"

Gabriel didn't have an answer to that. There was something good and right about Bluebird Hills—about the Amish way of life—but he had never been able to access it. He had always wanted it, though.

Now, it seemed, he was just as out of place among the *Englisch*.

The worst part was the guilt. He kept replaying the moment he had said goodbye to Aunt Mary. "I'm not giving up on you, Gabriel," she had said, tears sparkling in her eyes. Then, after he had turned his back to leave, she had whispered, "you can't let your *daed* control you forever."

He had spun around at that, eyes wide. "I'm

leaving. That means he's not controlling me anymore."

Mary had given a small, sad sigh. "*Ach*, Gabriel, if only that were true."

The church district was abuzz with whispers about Gabriel, though no one spoke about it directly to her. Eliza could sense the upheaval in the way people looked at his aunt Mary or shook their heads and clucked their tongues when his name was mentioned.

Eliza had returned to work now that he was gone, and the hours crept past with agonizing slowness. She missed his quick wit and playful smile. She missed the way he challenged her thinking and pushed her to let go and enjoy life.

But the more she thought about it, the more she felt betrayed and abandoned. That terrible question hung in the air as a dark, constant cloud.

Why hadn't he said goodbye?

Sure, she had pushed him away, communicated that she couldn't speak to him anymore. But if he really cared about her, he surely would have reached out one last time before he left. If only he had given her that chance, she might have been able to convince him to stay.

As she mulled it over Eliza realized that, when she stripped everything away, one fact remained: he chose to leave the faith, just like her mother had warned. The final straw came when Priss learned what had happened. Eliza had avoided telling her, hoping to put it off until she could handle it better. But a few days after Gabriel left, Eliza looked out the window of the gift shop to see Priss running through the south pasture that led to the one-room schoolhouse. Simon trotted behind her, barely able to keep up, a solemn frown on his little face. When Priss reached the fence to the farmyard, pushed it open and then slammed it behind her, Eliza could see the tear streaks on her cheeks.

Wiping her nose with her sleeve, Priss stumbled past the chickens and mud puddles, across the gravel parking lot, and up the wooden steps of the shop. Eliza met her at the door to crouch down and scoop her up into her arms. "What's wrong?"

Priss began to cry. She tried to speak, but the words came out in a jumble of hiccups and sobs. Simon slipped inside and quietly shut the door. Eliza turned her attention from Priss to Simon. "What's going on?"

He sighed and took off his straw hat. "We

heard something bad at school today," he said, scratching his head.

Eliza's heart sank. She knew what this must be about.

"Gabriel's gone," Priss said as she pressed her face into Eliza's shoulder.

Simon nodded and turned his hat in his hands. "I don't understand, Eliza. Why'd he leave? Doesn't he like us anymore?"

"If he liked us, he wouldn't have left us!" Priss shouted, the words muffled by Eliza's shoulder. Then she collapsed into deeper sobs.

"Shh." Eliza rubbed her hand in circles over Priss's back. "It's going to be *oll recht*."

"*Nee*, it can't be *oll recht*. Gabriel went *Englisch*, and that means he's never coming back. And I thought…"

Eliza felt her heart constrict as she held Priss tighter. "What did you think, sweetheart?"

"I thought he wanted to be my *daed*!"

Eliza felt the wind knock right out of her. She had been balanced on her heels, and she fell back onto her rear with a thud. "Your *daed*?" Her daughter had longed for Gabriel to join their family too. Of course she had. He would have been a wonderful father.

"But he didn't love me enough."

"*Nee!*" Eliza gripped Priss tighter. "This

has nothing to do with you. He and I weren't even courting. He couldn't be your *daed* if we weren't courting. You have to court before you get married, *ya?*"

"But he was going to court you!" Priss shrieked.

Simon agreed with a silent nod.

"*Nee.* If he were going to, he would have. He chose to leave, which means he was not interested in marrying me. I'm sure he would have loved to have been your *daed*, but he would have had to marry me to do that, and he didn't want to." Eliza wondered about her words, even as she said them. She had been the one to push him away. But he had been the one to leave. And if he had loved her—if he had actually wanted to marry her—he would have pushed back and tried to see her. He wouldn't have just agreed to leave her alone. He would have stayed; he would have fought for her.

Or at least given her a chance to say good-bye and explain herself before it was too late.

"But why did he leave?" Priss asked. She wiped her tears on Eliza's dress and pulled away to look her in the eyes.

Eliza exhaled as she considered her answer. There was only one thing to say: the truth. "He made a bad decision. He should not have left. It was irresponsible, and it hurt the people who love him."

"People like you and me?" Priss asked, her big brown eyes glistening with tears.

"Ya," Eliza said. "People like you and me."

"And me," Simon added quietly, his eyes on the floor.

Eliza had thought her heartbreak over Gabriel could not get any worse. But it just had. And that tipped the scales on her anger.

How dare Gabriel hurt Priss like this?

Gabriel slouched in a camping chair in his apartment, whittling a block of wood and listening to a man on television talk about the weather. A knock on the door startled him, and he dropped the knife in his hand. It skidded across the floor and bounced against the bare wall. Gabriel stood up quickly, wood shavings scattering from his lap. He hadn't had a visitor in days.

He opened the door to reveal Aunt Mary's tight face. She maintained an even expression, but he could see the pain in her eyes as she took in his empty apartment. *"Kumme* in." He stepped aside and motioned her inside. "Is everything *oll recht*?" He picked up the camping chair, shook out the wood shavings and set it back down. "Sit here. Sorry, it's all the furniture I have."

Mary shook her head. "*Nee,* I can't stay long. The *Englisch* driver I hired is waiting outside. I'm on my way back to the hospital."

Gabriel's stomach dropped. "The hospital? Who's at the hospital?" He reached out and gripped Mary's arms. "Not Eliza?" He shook his head, willing it not to be true.

"*Nee,* it's Priss," Mary said.

Gabriel sucked in his breath. *"Nee."*

"It's her appendix. Last I heard, they didn't know if they caught the infection in time. She woke up with a terrible bellyache, and by the time they got to the hospital…" Mary shook her head. "She was going into surgery when I left to *kumme* here."

"Let's go," Gabriel said. He led the way without looking back, not even taking the time to lock the door.

Gabriel braced himself before storming in through the hospital's automatic doors. He knew a lot of people from the church district would be there to support the Zooks, and he knew what they must think of him now. He tried to keep his emotions in check as he barreled down the stark-white hallway, his sneakers squeaking on the linoleum floor as Mary led the way to the waiting room.

Gabriel's heart jumped into his throat when they strode into a large room with a handful of *Englischers* in one corner and a crowd of men and women in Plain clothing filling the rest of the seats. It startled him to see so many straw hats and suspenders after his time away. Then he saw Eliza, and his heart leaped even higher until he felt it would pop right out of his body. Her hands were clasped tightly in her lap, her lips drawn into a thin line. Her big, round glasses obscured her eyes as she looked down. Then her eyes darted up and made contact with his. An emotion he couldn't quite read flicked across her face, then disappeared, replaced with hardness. She looked back down.

More than anything, he wanted to run to her, scoop her up in his arms and tell her that everything would be okay. He swallowed hard as he stared at the top of her head. She was making such a point of not looking at him that he couldn't even see her face. He glanced at Mary, and she gave a slight shake of the head. "Let her be," she whispered.

Regret swept over him in a hot wave.

Of all the scenarios he had imagined when he saw Eliza again, this was not one of them.

He should have realized that she would shun him after what he had done—not officially, of course, since he wasn't baptized—but in her heart. How could she do any less? He had left the faith, just as everyone had warned he would.

Gabriel stood for a long, awkward moment before turning away and finding a chair outside of the small crowd of Amish. Aunt Mary glanced at the group, then followed Gabriel. "You don't have to sit with me," he said in a tight voice as soon as she settled into the chair beside him.

"I want to," she answered quietly, then pulled a half-finished mitten and a ball of brown yarn from her bag.

They sat in silence for a while. Gabriel tried not to look at Eliza, but his gaze kept wandering back to her. He shifted in the uncomfortable plastic chair and sighed.

"I've missed you," Mary said finally, eyes on her knitting needles.

Gabriel closed his eyes and leaned his head against the wall. "I'm sorry," he whispered. "I guess I proved everyone right."

"That's not what I meant." Mary's knitting needles clicked. "I just wanted you to know I miss you. That's all."

Gabriel hesitated. "I miss you too."

Mary nodded. The room was silent except for the clatter of knitting needles and the low murmur of voices across the room. "I'm not the only one, you know."

"No one wants anything to do with me now." Gabriel opened his eyes and looked at Eliza. She was still sitting with her hands clasped in her lap, her face a quiet mask.

"I don't know about that," Mary said.

"I do." Gabriel caught movement out of the corner of his eye, turned his head and saw Viola Esch stand up from her seat. She patted Lovina's hand, said something to her that Gabriel couldn't make out and then shuffled toward Gabriel. He braced himself for whatever she was about to say. It felt like it took forever for her to cross the room as she leaned on her cane, taking each step slowly and carefully. He had plenty of time to imagine the browbeating she was about to give him.

But when she reached him, Viola just shook her head and lowered herself onto the seat beside him. "Finally jumped the fence, *ya*?"

"Ya." He looked down at his hands. He was already losing some of the calluses from his farmwork.

"Regret it yet?"

Gabriel could feel Viola's sharp, discerning stare even though his eyes were down. He thought about his cramped, empty apartment; the strange, silent faces at work; the impersonal parking lot that surrounded his apartment. "*Nee*. It's for the best."

"Pfffft."

Gabriel glanced up in time to see Viola roll her eyes. "Stop that nonsense. You know as well as I do that you've made a mistake. You don't belong out there with the *Englisch*."

Gabriel flexed his jaw but didn't respond.

"You don't belong there," she repeated, tapping the floor with her cane for emphasis.

"Tell that to them," he said and swept his arm toward the Amish in the row of seats across the room.

"They know you better than you know yourself?"

Gabriel started to respond, then shook his head. He threw up his hands. "Maybe."

Viola rolled her eyes again. "Time to get some sense, Gabriel, before it's too late. At your age, people think they have all the time in the world—time to make mistakes, time to make it right again—but it doesn't always work that way." She narrowed her eyes, picked up her cane and pointed it at him. "*Gott* has a plan for you, and you best see it through. Don't wait until it's too late. There are people here who need you."

"I know. Don't you think I feel guilty enough about leaving *Aenti* Mary as it is?"

Viola raised her eyebrows. "I'm not talking about Mary."

Gabriel flinched. "Who…"

Viola gave him a look that showed he ought to know the answer to that question.

Gabriel didn't respond. He had no idea what to say. Then Eliza rose from her seat across the room, taking Gabriel's attention away from Viola. Lovina handed Eliza a few bills and said something to her; then Eliza walked across the room, toward the door. She looked so small and vulnerable, even though she managed to keep that stoic expression on her face. Gabriel watched her disappear into the hallway, his heart aching to follow.

Viola nudged Gabriel with her cane.

He jumped and flicked his attention to her.

"Well? What are you waiting for?"

He frowned at Viola.

"Go after her."

Gabriel exhaled.

"Viola's right," Mary said. "Go."

Gabriel nodded, gathered his courage and rose to his feet.

Chapter Fifteen

Eliza stared at the vending machine. Lovina wanted her to eat, but she wasn't hungry. She rubbed a dollar bill between her fingers as she studied the packages of chips, crackers and candy. When she heard footsteps behind her, she frowned and pushed a button. "Sorry, I'll just be a second."

"Take your time," a deep, familiar voice answered.

Eliza nearly spun around to launch herself into Gabriel's arms. But she caught herself and froze. Her heart raced and her eyes burned. Seconds passed. She could feel a tremor moving through her as she forced herself not to turn around.

"Eliza?" His voice was soft, pleading.

She shook her head. "Don't."

"I just… I just want to tell you I'm sorry."

"Oll recht. You've said it." She tried to study the vending machine buttons, but the sound of Gabriel's breath distracted her. She hit another random button. A number blinked on the display, and she fed the dollar bill into the slot. Her eyes blurred, but she refused to wipe them. She would not let Gabriel know how much he had hurt her.

"How is Priss?"

"I don't know." A series of thumps sounded deep inside the vending machine, followed by a thud as something dropped. Eliza pushed her hand inside and pulled out a bag of chocolate candies. She sighed; it wasn't what she'd wanted.

None of this was what she wanted.

Eliza spun around to face Gabriel. She looked up at his face, opened her mouth to berate him, but was thrown by his strange *Englisch* haircut. "What have you done to yourself?" she asked.

Gabriel's hand flew to his hair. *"Ach,* this?" He shrugged. "You don't like it?"

"You look ridiculous," Eliza said.

Gabriel sighed. His eyes looked sad. *"Ya."*

Eliza didn't like this sad, cowed version of Gabriel. She wanted him to push back. She shook her head. "What have you done?" Her voice sounded sharper than she meant it to.

"It's only hair. It'll grow back."

"I'm not talking about your hair."

Gabriel looked down. He shifted his weight from one foot to the other. "I didn't mean to hurt you."

"Well, you did. You proved my mother right—you proved all of them right. How could you?" Eliza realized she couldn't stop now that she had started. All the fear she had been feeling for Priss, all the pain she had been pushing down about Gabriel—it all came flying out. "You asked how Priss is, so I'll tell you. She's heartbroken. She wanted you to be her *daed*." Eliza snorted and planted her hands on her hips. "Can you believe that? She actually thought—" Eliza realized what she was saying and clamped her mouth shut. "Never mind. Forget I said anything. It's not as if you care, anyway." Eliza pushed past Gabriel, and he darted aside to let her by. She did not look back, but she could feel his eyes following her and knew he was watching her until she turned the corner and marched down the long, empty hallway alone.

The minutes crawled past as Eliza sat in the waiting room, the unopened bag of candy crumpled in her hand. People shuffled past periodically to offer a hug and a reassuring word, but Eliza felt too numb to respond. She could not think straight until she knew that Priss was going to be okay.

And to make matters worse, Gabriel sat on the other side of the room, stoically waiting for news even though Eliza had made it clear that he was unwanted. She regretted how harsh she had been to him when they spoke. But the thought of telling him how she really felt left a confusing ache in her chest. She wished he would leave.

She wished he would stay.

The war inside her was too much to handle on top of her worry over Priss, so she did nothing. Perhaps then, the problem would simply go away.

"Eliza Zook?" a voice asked from the doorway.

Eliza stumbled to her feet when she saw the middle-aged man in a white coat scanning the room. "That's me."

The man nodded, glanced at a clipboard in his hand and then looked back to Eliza. "Priscilla is going to be fine. It was a close call, but we caught the infection in time. She should make a full recovery without complications."

Sighs of relief and murmurs of "Praise *Gott*" rippled through the small crowd of Amish. Eliza's knees felt weak. "Can I see her?"

"Yes."

Lovina leaped up to follow Eliza, Viola Esch trailing not far behind. Eliza couldn't help but notice Gabriel as she swept past him. The relief was evident on his face, and his lips were moving in a silent prayer of thanks. Seeing the genuine emotion he had for Priss sent a pang through her heart. She clenched her fists to keep from reaching out to him. She had to be strong for Priss. She had to remember that Gabriel could not be trusted, no matter how much he seemed to care.

When they reached Priss's room, the doctor turned and frowned. "Family only," he said.

"We're *all* family," Viola said and barged through the door. Lovina kept walking. The doctor looked to Eliza and she nodded.

"Big family, huh? I guess that's common with the Amish?"

Eliza was not sure how to answer. "We are all very close," she said after a slight hesitation. Viola was not related to them and Eliza would not lie, but what she said was true. The entire church district was like one big family.

They celebrated together, mourned together, supported one another through thick and thin.

Even Gabriel, who wasn't even part of the church district anymore, had shown up to give his support. These were bonds that could not be broken, even when someone wanted to break them. The realization churned within her as she ran to Priss, took the child's warm hand in hers and kissed her cool forehead.

The hours moved slowly as Eliza waited for Priss to recover. She was too thankful to mind the wait, although her fingers itched to stay busy. She wished she had brought her knitting, but that had been the last thing on her mind when they rushed to the hospital early that morning. Finally, she took Viola's advice to take a walk around the hallways.

"You're not doing any good sitting here," Viola said to her and Lovina. "Priss is asleep and she needs her rest. You should both take a break."

Eliza and Lovina wandered the hospital for a while, observing the people in fancy clothes and flashy hairstyles and listening to the echo of their footsteps along the long, silent corridors. But they didn't want to stay away long, and they soon headed back to Priss's room. As they neared the door, Eliza could hear the low rumble of a man's voice from inside. Her pulse quickened when she realized she had missed the doctor's update. She should not have left, no matter what Viola said.

But when Eliza pushed the door open, she saw Gabriel sitting on the edge of the bed, a soft smile on his face, while Priss laughed. Her eyes shone and her cheeks had regained some of their color.

"Gabriel?" Eliza asked, her voice wavering.

Lovina's mouth tightened into a straight line.

Gabriel's smile dropped. He cleared his throat and stood up.

"Gabriel's back!" Priss said with a grin.

"I'm so happy to see you're feeling better," Eliza said, carefully avoiding any mention of Gabriel.

Lovina was much more direct. "I think it's best you leave," Lovina said to him.

"Look what *gut* he's done," Viola said.

Lovina and Viola exchanged an irritated glance with each other. "You can't tell me I'm wrong, Lovina." Viola raised her eyebrows as she kept her eyes locked on Lovina.

Lovina dropped her gaze first. Her lips puckered as if she had eaten a lemon.

Gabriel could clearly sense the tension in the room. "I, uh, better let you sleep," he said to Priss, then gave her a quick pat on the head and hurried to the door. He hesitated, turned back around to nod to Viola and then looked at Eliza. "I'm sorry for intruding. I just had to see that she was okay with my own eyes."

"You've seen her now," Eliza said.

Gabriel's face crumpled. He glanced back at Priss, forced a smile and an exaggerated wave, then walked away.

Eliza wanted to run after him. He had been so good with Priss. But as sweet as he was with her, his lifestyle would lead her astray. Eliza had to stay firm, no matter how much it hurt.

"You did the right thing," Lovina said. "Not you, Viola. I'm talking to my *dochter*."

Viola grunted. "Never seen such a stubborn woman."

"Then you should look in the mirror," Lovina said.

"That boy has a *gut* heart," Viola said, tapping her cane on the floor to emphasize the word *gut*.

"Then he should act like it," Lovina said.

Priss looked at the adults in the room with big, confused eyes. "He was," she said in a small, sober voice. "He made me feel better."

The three women fell silent. None of them could argue that—not even Lovina.

* * *

Gabriel did not intrude again, but he didn't leave the hospital either. He stayed in the waiting room until Priss was released. She caught a glimpse of him as they wheeled her past the open door, broke into a big smile and waved. Gabriel grinned and returned the wave. He wanted to follow her to the hired *Englisch* car and make her laugh one more time, but he forced himself to stay back out of respect for Eliza's wishes.

Eliza did not turn her head as she followed the nurse pushing Priss's wheelchair past the waiting room, but he could sense that she noticed him when her posture stiffened. Lovina acknowledged him with a glare, then turned her nose up and kept walking. Gabriel sighed.

He was the only person left in the waiting room. Everyone else had left when they heard Priss would be okay. The men had to take care of their chores, and the women had gone to Mary's for a work frolic to prepare a few meals for the Zooks. Gabriel could imagine the happy clang of pots and pans in Mary's kitchen and the quiet murmur of chatter as the womenfolk worked. He longed to be there, smelling the roasting meat and sugary pies, feeling like he was one of the group.

Except he wasn't.

And that had been painfully evident the entire time he had been in the waiting room. Mary and Viola had supported him, and Katie had offered a kind hello, but most of the crowd had just stared at him, then turned away. Even the bishop had looked at him with disappointed eyes while trying to offer some encouragement to return.

Worst of all was the look on Eliza's face and the tone in her voice when she had spoken to him. She wanted nothing to do with him anymore.

Before Mary had left to host the work frolic, she turned to Gabriel, squeezed his hand and asked, "Won't you *kumme* back?"

He had sighed and looked down. "*Nee.* I don't belong. Can't you see that?"

Her eyes had moved to the row of stern, disapproving faces across the room. She had hesitated, then nodded and said, "I'm always here if you change your mind."

"It's not *my* mind that needs changing," he had said.

"You've become a self-fulfilling prophecy that your *daed* set in motion," she had replied.

Gabriel had just shrugged. "Regardless, it's done."

That conversation kept playing in his head. Because he was right—it was done. There was no way he could face the community now, even if he wanted to go back. It was best not to think about it and to just keep moving forward with his new life.

When Gabriel returned to his apartment, he missed the sound of chickens in the yard, the low mooing of cattle, the squeak of the Millers' metal windmill in the breeze. Most of all, he missed the easy camaraderie that came with living in a place that had been home for years. Everyone had known him in Bluebird Hills. He could speak to anyone, at any time.

But wasn't that the problem? Everyone knew him, so they knew his faults. They knew he would never live up to the community's expectations. Gabriel flicked on the electric lights, hung his house key on the hook by the door and collapsed into his camping chair. He turned on the television for company and listened to a stranger's voice as she demonstrated a recipe for chocolate chip cookies. That made him think about Eliza and the molasses cookies that she had baked for him. He wished he was back home, laughing with her in the gift shop, nibbling a cookie, just enjoying the moment.

For an instant he entertained the idea. What

if he just packed up and went home right now? He could be back in his warm, comfortable bed in Mary's house tonight. Tomorrow morning he could wander downstairs to a home-cooked breakfast of eggs, bacon and coffee cake. He could go back to the Miller farm, see Eliza…

Gabriel sighed. No. That was just a fantasy. Eliza would not see him. He wasn't even sure the Millers would take him back after he had let them down.

There was no going home.

Eliza was torn between joy at Priss's recovery and angst at seeing Gabriel again. Why did he have to be so kind and thoughtful? It would be so much easier if he would be completely bad. But instead, he still acted like the father she had always wanted for Priss. He comforted the child and made her laugh, even in the midst of a near tragedy. The doctor had explained that it might have been too late if they had waited any longer to get to the hospital. Every time Eliza thought about that, she wanted to turn to Gabriel and tell him how she felt. Then she caught herself and realized she would never tell him anything again.

Lovina carefully avoided the subject of Gabriel over the next few days, and Eliza wondered what her mother was thinking. Priss, on the other hand, could not stop talking about him. "Will he visit me?" she asked as Eliza sat on the edge of her bed. "I've been home three days, and he hasn't *kumme* to see me yet. When is he coming?"

A fresh wave of sadness rippled through Eliza. "He can't *kumme* back," she said, reaching down to move a strand of brown hair from Priss's face.

Priss looked confused. "Why not? He came to see me at the hospital."

"I know…" Eliza bit her lip. "That was different."

"How?"

Eliza tucked the quilt beneath Priss's chin and smoothed out the wrinkles with the palm of her hand.

"How?" Priss repeated.

"It just was."

Priss crinkled her forehead. "I don't think so."

Eliza sighed. She didn't have a good explanation.

"Go to sleep," Eliza said and clicked off the battery-powered lamp beside the bed. "You still need lots of rest."

Priss snuggled deeper beneath the quilt and

closed her eyes. *"Ya,"* she murmured. "But I'm not giving up on Gabriel."

The little girl's steadfast faith struck Eliza with the force of a thunderclap.

"And neither should you," Priss continued. *"Gott* never would, ain't so?"

Eliza didn't answer. She just stared at Priss, wondering at the little girl's simple wisdom.

Priss's eyes opened when Eliza didn't respond. "Ain't so?"

"Ya," Eliza answered quietly. "You're right. *Gott* has not given up on Gabriel." *So why have I?*

A rush of emotion surged through Eliza, and she pressed her hand against the wall to brace herself. Why had she spent so much time listening to her mother—and anyone else with a strong opinion—instead of the only opinion that really mattered?

Why hadn't she listened to her heart all this time? Hadn't she known, deep down, that Gabriel was a *gut* man who just needed someone to believe in him? Images of Gabriel with Priss ran through her mind. She remembered the remorse and regret in his eyes when he cornered her at the vending machine. Would he have even left if she had not pushed him away that last day in the shop?

No, he would not have left. He had wanted to stay.

Suddenly, Eliza felt an explosion of self-confidence that she had never felt before. She had known the truth all along. The surety zipped through her like lightening, making her fingers and toes tingle. She knew just as much as her mother when it came to matters of the heart—and when it came to Gabriel, she knew more than Lovina. Eliza had the right to be the authority of her own feelings and relationships, no matter what anyone else thought.

Eliza pushed away from the wall and hurried out of the room, heart racing. She didn't have a moment to lose.

Lovina jumped up from the sofa as Eliza rushed through the living room. "I'll be back later," Eliza said over her shoulder and kept moving. She could hear her mother's footsteps following her into the entry hall. Eliza's hand trembled as she reached for the doorknob.

Lovina slid between Eliza and the front door.

"At this hour?" Lovina frowned and folded her arms across her chest. "What are you doing?"

"What I should have done a long time ago," Eliza answered.

"And what, exactly, is that?"

"The right thing."

"*Ach*, Eliza, stop talking in circles and speak plainly. I have a pretty *gut* idea what's on your mind, you know."

Eliza straightened to her full height. "I'm going to make things right with Gabriel."

Lovina made a noise in the back of her throat. "We've talked about this, Eliza."

"*Nee, you've* talked and I've listened. All these years, I've listened and done as you've said. I've honored you as the scriptures say I should. But it has never been enough for you."

Lovina's brow slammed down. "After all I've—"

Eliza held up a hand. "Nee, *Mamm*. It's my turn to talk. I know Rebekah broke your heart—she broke mine too. But I'm not Rebekah. Neither is Priss. And treating us the same way you treated Rebekah isn't going to keep us Amish. We're going to choose this way of life because it's the right way, not because you force us into it."

"I never forced—"

"Through guilt, *Mamm*. Through meddling with every detail of our lives. You have to let us go in order to keep us."

Lovina took a shaky breath. "I never..." She shook her head and didn't finish the sentence.

"I know you never meant any harm. I know you're only trying to protect us. But you're the one who always says the road to wickedness is paved with *gut* intentions."

"I never meant that about me!"

Eliza gave her mother a level look. "Does that make a difference?"

Lovina sagged against the wall. Her face looked ashen. Eliza grabbed her mother's elbow and steered her to the nearest chair. "Sit," Eliza ordered. "I'll get you a glass of water." Eliza glanced at the clock on the wall. It was getting late, and everything in her burned to get to Gabriel.

"Nee."

"It'll help. You look faint."

"Water won't help."

Eliza braced herself. "Then what will?"

Lovina turned away. "I don't know." She shook her head. "Why haven't you said anything before? You've felt this way all this time?"

"Ya, Mamm," Eliza said gently. "All this time." She stepped closer to Lovina's chair. "But I couldn't say anything."

Lovina's eyes snapped to her daughter, and her face took on an irritated glare. "Why not?"

Eliza gave her a steady, even look that held

more power than she knew she possessed. "Because you wouldn't let me."

The room fell silent. The second hand on the battery-powered clock ticked. A car engine rumbled in the distance.

"Is this what you call honoring your mother?" Lovina asked at last.

Eliza raised her chin. "*Ya.* It is. Telling the truth is honoring you, *Mamm.* Taking the path *Gott* has for me is honoring you. Enabling your fear does not honor you. It only hurts you— hurts all of us. I just wish I'd realized that sooner." She thought about Gabriel and how he'd had to walk away from his father. "Honor does not always mean obedience. Not when that obedience goes against *Gott's* ways."

"And how do you know what *Gott's* ways are?" Lovina asked with a pointed look.

"Because I know *Gott,*" Eliza said simply. "And I know Gabriel too."

Lovina didn't answer. She stared into the middle distance, her jaw slack. Eliza had never seen her look so old. "Just go," Lovina whispered.

"You're telling me to go?" Eliza leaned closer.

"*Nee.* But I can't stop you." Lovina hesitated. "And maybe…maybe I shouldn't." She shook her head, still refusing to look at Eliza.

"I don't know anymore. So just go." Her voice strengthened with the last sentence.

Eliza swallowed and backed away. "*Oll recht, Mamm.* I'll go." But her feet would not move. "Are you sure you're okay?"

Lovina nodded and motioned toward the door. Eliza knew she was running out of time if she was going to leave tonight. Her heart could not bear to wait until morning. For the first time in her life, she was going to follow that cry from deep within.

Eliza escaped through the front door and shut it firmly behind her. She shivered in the cool night air and hugged herself as she set off down the road. A few cars grumbled past, but the neighborhood was mostly still and quiet. Moonlight shone down on the row of brick houses and the long stretch of black pavement. Eliza's pulse pounded with each step that took her closer to her purpose.

She reached the phone shanty they shared with the rest of the block and dialed the number of her *Englisch* driver with shaky fingers. "I'm sorry to call so late," she said in a rush. "Can you give me a ride now?"

"Sure," her teenage driver, Scott, said. "Wouldn't mind making a little money."

"I didn't wake you?" Eliza asked.

Scott chuckled. "Nope. I was just binge-watching Netflix. It's only ten thirty, you know."

"Right." Eliza always forgot that electricity kept the *Englisch* up late.

"Be there in a minute," Scott said before the line went dead, and Eliza was left staring at the empty street through the dusty window of the phone shanty. The only sound was the thud of her heart in her ears as she prayed she wasn't too late.

Eliza had heard where Gabriel was living; word spread fast through the church district. While the *Englisch* had Netflix to keep them entertained, the Amish relied on information about one another to pass the time. So she knew where to tell Scott to go when he arrived. The drive was only about fifteen minutes, but Gabriel's apartment was a world away. Her stomach dropped when she saw the dingy complex overlooking an impersonal-looking shopping center. This was nothing like the quaint row of shops in Bluebird Hills' little downtown, where she knew all the shop-keepers and could expect to run into a friend on every corner.

"You want me to wait?" Scott asked as he pulled into a parking space.

Eliza studied the building's peeling blue paint, empty concrete stairwells and metal fire escapes. What if this didn't go as planned? Her stomach tightened with trepidation. "*Ya*. Just for a minute."

"Gotcha." Scott turned off the engine, then picked up his smartphone and swiped across the screen.

Eliza pushed the door open and climbed out of the car. She didn't know whether to be excited or scared. She flexed her fingers, walked up to the door marked "124," took a deep breath and knocked. For a moment, a flash of fear shot through her. *I'm going against everything I've always believed.*

Eliza squeezed her eyes shut and tightened her fists. "Please, *Gott*, help me to do the right thing." Renewed confidence filled her. She knew she wasn't going against her beliefs— she was keeping them, even if no one but her could see that.

The door did not open.

Eliza knocked again. No lights flicked on inside the apartment. The windows remained dark, the night air silent and still. Eliza glanced back at the car behind her. The bright headlights shone in her eyes, forcing her gaze downward.

The window rolled down in a soft whir and the low beat of a bass guitar filled the silence. "Want me to take you back home now?" Scott asked.

Eliza turned her attention down the long, lonely parking lot and braced herself. "No. I know where to try next."

She was not giving up.

Chapter Sixteen

Gabriel wiped moisture from his face with the back of his hand, then squeezed the nozzle to release another blast of hot water into the sink full of crusted dishes. Bright lights and noise filled the overheated room as co-workers shouted above the clang and bang of the kitchen. Gabriel glanced at the clock. Nearly 11:00 p.m., and he was still working. Back home, he would be sound asleep beneath a warm, soft quilt so he could get up with the sun to feed the stock. But here, among the *Englisch*, people worked odd hours—all night, sometimes—as if the natural rhythm of the sun didn't exist. The change of schedule exhausted him. His body knew it wasn't right.

But he had no choice but to press on. If the *Englisch* wanted to eat supper at eleven at night, then he had to wash their dishes to pay his rent and keep his electricity running, no matter how much he wanted to go home and crawl into bed. He tried to block out the harsh sounds that filled the kitchen and focus on getting the job done until he could leave.

"Hey, Gabriel!" a voice called out from across the room.

"Ya?" Gabriel flinched. He had to stop using Pennsylvania Dutch, but that was like trying to remember not to breathe—it just came naturally, without thinking. "Yeah?" he corrected himself.

"Someone's here to see you. You can take your break now."

Gabriel frowned and wiped his hands on a white bar cloth beside the sink. A visitor was the last thing he expected. Maybe one of his *Englisch* acquaintances wanted to convince him to go out drinking after work, but he doubted it. He had refused enough times by now that they didn't bother coming around anymore. Worry nipped at his heels as he hurried across the kitchen, through the double doors and across the restaurant to the alcove, where diners waited to be seated.

Gabriel skidded to a stop and froze. Eliza stood in front of him, looking as neat and prim as ever in her starched heart-shaped prayer *kapp*, emerald green cape dress, neatly ironed apron and sensible black athletic shoes. She looked completely out of place against the dingy walls, loud jukebox music and glare of the overhead light.

"Hello, Gabriel," she said.

He stared back at her.

"Aren't you going to say anything?" The hint of a smile played on her lips.

Gabriel swallowed hard. "Hello?" He ran his fingers through his hair as he studied her expression. "Why are you here?"

"I've *kumme* to take you home, Gabriel King."

"You've what?"

"I've *kumme* to take you home," Eliza repeated.

Gabriel glanced behind him. Was this some kind of strange joke? No, Eliza would never participate in a joke like that. She was too straight laced for such foolishness. In fact, she was too straightlaced to be here, at a seedy twenty-four-hour diner, for any reason at all. "You shouldn't be here," Gabriel said.

A shadow passed over Eliza's face; then she set her jaw and lifted her chin. "You don't want me here?"

Gabriel shook his head. "I just mean that you don't belong here. This isn't a place I ever expected to see you…"

"So you do want me here." She gave him an even, steady stare that made Gabriel look away. He licked his lips, then forced his gaze back to hers. *"Ya,"* he said softly. "I do want you here." He furrowed his brow. *"Nee.* I don't. I want to be with you somewhere else. This place…" He made a dismissive gesture toward the crowd behind him. "It isn't a *gut* place for you." He swallowed hard. "Or for me."

"I just heard you say you want to be with me."

Gabriel felt the air thicken around him. He couldn't get enough breath. "Let's go outside. I need some air." He pushed open the door, held it for her and followed her into the cool, crisp night air. Neon lights cast a pink glow over a sidewalk littered with cigarette butts and aluminum cans. The music faded into a distant thud of drums and bass guitar as the door closed behind them.

Gabriel's heart hammered inside his chest as he exhaled and turned to face Eliza. Her expression was smooth and confident. He wasn't sure what she wanted to hear. "I don't know what to say."

"You've said a lot already. May as well finish what you started."

"I didn't mean to say anything."

"But you did. Now, tell me the truth. Do you want to be with me or not?"

Gabriel felt the fight disappear from him, like a balloon deflating. He could not run or hide the truth anymore. "*Ya.* I do. I think about you every day. I want to be together again, like we were." He shifted his weight from one foot to the other and looked down at the grimy sidewalk. "But more. I want to be more than friends." He glanced back up at her, his body clenched with fear at what her expression would be.

She pushed her glasses up her nose and smiled. "*Gut.* Because I feel the same way about you."

"But…" Gabriel held up his hands. "I left. I don't understand how you can feel the same way after I let you down."

"I didn't stop loving you just because you left." Eliza's eyes widened for an instant; then she winced and looked away.

"Now who's the one who said more than they meant to say?" Gabriel asked gently.

Eliza clapped her hand over her face. "Please

forget I said that. I don't know how that slipped out."

"I hope the reason it slipped out is because it's true." He stepped closer to her and grasped the hand she was holding over her face to hide herself from him. He slowly lowered her hand. Her skin felt warm and right against his. His eyes focused on hers and held her gaze. "Because I love you too."

Eliza inhaled sharply. She blinked a few times and stared up at him. He had never seen anything as adorable as Eliza Zook gazing at him through her big, round glasses in that moment, her eyes full of hope and amazement.

It took a few beats for Eliza to gather herself. Then she raised her chin a fraction and said, "You'll have to leave all this. We can't be together as long as you're on the wrong side of the fence."

Gabriel grinned, then reached up with his free hand to smooth the plane of her cheekbone with the back of his hand. "That's the Eliza I know and love."

"So you'll *kumme* home?" Her eyes locked on his.

"Of course I will."

"Just like that?" Eliza's brow crinkled. "I thought I would have to talk sense into you."

Gabriel shrugged and gave a sheepish smile. "All I ever wanted was to belong somewhere. And now I do. With you."

Her eyes narrowed. "You'll get baptized and commit fully to the faith?"

"*Ya*. I will."

A long, happy sigh escaped Eliza's lips, and her shoulders sagged with relief. "Gabriel, I was so afraid…" Her eyes watered as she shook her head. "I didn't think you'd be willing. You've always felt so rejected by the community." She collapsed into his chest, the weight of her worry evaporating.

Gabriel wrapped his arms around her and kissed the top of her head. She smelled faintly of chamomile and sun-dried laundry. He wanted this moment to last forever. He finally held the woman who had become home to him—the woman who had always been there but whom he had never noticed before she burst into his life to stop a runaway horse. No one had ever been so full of surprises as Eliza Zook. She, of all people, had shown him the road to acceptance.

"*Ya*," he answered after breathing her in for a good, long moment. "I've felt rejected. But after I left, that feeling of rejection didn't go away. I just felt lost and bewildered by my new life on top of feeling rejected. But I didn't feel like I could go back, because everyone was so disappointed in me. I could see it in their eyes at the hospital. I couldn't face them."

"And now you can?" Her fingers tightened around his sleeve, refusing to let him go.

"*Ya.* Because if you can accept me, then I know anyone can."

Eliza laughed into his chest, his shirt muffling the sound. "That's the silliest logic I ever heard."

"But it's true. No one holds a higher standard than Eliza Zook."

Eliza pulled away from him to see his face. Her expression looked troubled. "I never meant to make you feel like you had to live up to an impossible standard. I never expected more from you—or anyone else—than I expected from myself."

"And what do you expect from yourself?"

Eliza bit her lip. "Perfection," she said after a moment's hesitation.

"You know that's impossible, *ya*?"

"I do now. Because you've shown me I'm *gut* enough just as I am, even if I fall short sometimes." Her voice wavered with emotion. "Otherwise, you wouldn't love me. Because I haven't been perfect around you, that's for certain sure."

"No one can ever be perfect," Gabriel said. "But you are perfect for me." And then he leaned down and kissed her gently, but with all the emotion overflowing within him, so she understood exactly how much she meant to him.

Epilogue

Gabriel and Eliza went straight to her house to face Lovina with their hands held together tightly, both of them standing with spines straight, defiant in their resolve. Every muscle in Eliza's body tensed as she waited for the fallout.

But Lovina just shook her head and threw up her hands. "What can I do but bless this?"

"Bless this?" Eliza sputtered, then exchanged a glance with Gabriel. She wondered if her mother had lost her mind. Maybe she had pushed her too far earlier that night.

"I told you that Gabriel had proven himself to be a bad influence when he left. Well, doesn't that mean he's proven his *gut* intentions by returning? How can I set myself against a man who has committed himself to the faith?" She narrowed her eyes. "You *will* be baptized, *ya*?"

"Just as soon as Bishop Amos will do it. I'd do it tonight, if I could."

Lovina gave a nod of approval.

"You're really okay with this?" Eliza asked.

Lovina sighed, then shrugged. "Not entirely. It'll take some time to change my ways." She stopped and wagged a finger at them. "And I'm not changing all of them. But I've been thinking about what you said to me earlier tonight. And even before you confronted me, I'd noticed how *gut* Gabriel is with Priss. After he jumped the fence, he was still so *gut* to her at the hospital. The only problem was his lack of commitment to our ways. It troubled me more and more to insist he stay away, but what else could I do? He left the faith, and I couldn't let him drag my *dochder* and *kinnskind* with him."

"Your heart was in the right place," Gabriel said. "I can't blame you for that reasoning. The truth is, I needed to figure out my place with *Gott* before I could figure out my relationship with Eliza or anyone else."

"As long as you get that right, everything else will fall into place," Lovina said. She hesitated, then cleared her throat. "I owe you an apology, Eliza. And you, too, Gabriel. I should have been more understanding."

Gabriel looked like a great weight had lifted from his shoulders with that one simple statement.

A thoughtful expression came over Lovina's face. "This is going to go a long way toward healing the loss our family has known. Seeing you *kumme* back to the faith makes me think I can believe for more than I ever thought possible."

Eliza reached out and squeezed her mother's arm as the emotions overflowed between them. Then Priss bounded into the room and rushed straight to Gabriel. "I knew I heard voices!" She leaped into his arms, and the conversation was lost to shouts and laughter.

"Does this mean that you're going to be my *daed*?" Priss asked, her big brown eyes full of hope.

"Ya," Gabriel said as he swung her onto his shoulders. "I'm going to marry your *mamm*." He and Eliza locked eyes, and a deep, unspoken understanding passed between them.

Facing the rest of the church district wasn't easy, but Eliza held Gabriel's hand every step of the way. Her steadfast support filled him with a courage he had never had before. If she believed in him even while he was living outside the faith, then he knew he could handle whatever waited for him when he returned.

What surprised Gabriel the most was the way the church district welcomed him back, especially after he publicly announced his decision to commit to the faith. He had never seen the bishop's eyes dance the way they did on the day of his baptism. "We never stopped believing in you, Gabriel," Amos whispered after the ceremony. "No matter what you thought." Warmth filled the air between them, and Gabriel had to look away as moisture filled his eyes.

The Millers gave him his old job back. Aunt Mary cried and said she knew he would come home again. She had kept his room exactly as he had left it. Viola Esch made a point to come over and say, "I told you so," while looking at him with satisfaction. She had known all along that he belonged in Bluebird Hills.

The marriage ceremony took place during the wedding season that fall. The Millers' house overflowed with cakes, pies, celery stalks and warm, excited smiles. The expectation in the air was palpable throughout the service as they all waited for the end, when the vows would be exchanged. Priss was the most eager, and Lovina had to give her more than one look to encourage her to stop wriggling while Bishop Amos preached a good, long sermon about the return of the prodigal son. Even Lovina began to look a little impatient by the end, though she hid it well.

Gabriel and Eliza kept stealing glances at each other from across the room. Neither one could stop grinning. Before Gabriel had come into her life, Eliza never would have dared to grin like that during a service.

But now she knew it was okay to live a little.

Gabriel, on the other hand, showed a seriousness he never had before Eliza came into his life. He was still quick to smile, but he was also quick to listen, and his attention usually stayed on Amos during his long sermons—except for today, when Gabriel was filled with eagerness at the thought of a life spent together with Eliza in Bluebird Hills.

When they finally stood in front of the long rows of benches, Eliza's small hand in his, Gabriel's heart felt so full he thought he might burst. They said their vows, then turned to look out over the congregation. Gabriel recognized every face. He knew the details of each life, cherished every journey.

Gabriel squeezed Eliza's hand and smiled in amazement. They were a family now. All of them. And he would always belong, no matter what.

* * * * *

Dear Reader,

I am so glad you have visited Bluebird Hills with me! Eliza's and Gabriel's story is one of my favorites. I have a weakness for a plot with a handsome, rebellious hero who the heroine believes is out of her league—until he falls for her because he recognizes her value, when other people around her haven't.

Isn't that what love is all about?

I hope that you feel truly valued for who you are, just like Eliza and Gabriel eventually do. It's not easy—and I'm certainly still working on it myself—but learning to love who God made you to be, regardless of how others see you, is one of the greatest gifts you can give yourself.

And look for the next book in Bluebird Hills, coming soon!

Love always,
Virginia.

COMING NEXT MONTH FROM
Love Inspired

THEIR AMISH SECRET
Amish Country Matches • by Patricia Johns

Putting the past behind her is all single Amish mother Claire Glick wants. But when old love Joel Beiler shows up on her doorstep in the middle of a harrowing storm, it could jeopardize everything she's worked for—including her best-kept secret...

THE QUILTER'S SCANDALOUS PAST
by Patrice Lewis

Esther Yoder's family must sell their mercantile store, and when an out-of-town buyer expresses interest, Esther is thrilled. Then she learns the buyer is Joseph Kemp—the man responsible for ruining her reputation. Can she set aside her feelings for the sake of the deal?

THE RANCHER'S SANCTUARY
K-9 Companions • by Linda Goodnight

With zero ranching experience, greenhorn Nathan Garrison has six months to reopen an abandoned guest ranch—or lose it forever. So he hires scarred cowgirl Monroe Matheson to show him the ropes. As they work together, will secrets from the past ruin their chance at love?

THE BABY INHERITANCE
Lazy M Ranch • by Tina Radcliffe

Life changes forever when rancher Drew Morgan inherits his best friend's baby. But when he learns professor Sadie Ross is also part of the deal, things get complicated. Neither one of them is ready for domestic bliss, but sweet baby Mae might change their minds...

MOTHER FOR A MONTH
by Zoey Marie Jackson

Career-weary Sienna King yearns to become a mother, and opportunity knocks when know-it-all reporter Joel Armstrong comes to her with an unusual proposal. Putting aside their differences, they must work together to care for his infant nephew, but what happens when their pretend family starts to feel real?

THE NANNY NEXT DOOR
Second Chance Blessings • by Jenna Mindel

Grieving widower Jackson Taylor moves to small-town Michigan for the sake of his girls. When he hires his attractive next-door neighbor, Maddie Williams, to be their nanny, it could be more than he bargained for as the line between personal and professional starts to blur...

LOOK FOR THESE AND OTHER LOVE INSPIRED BOOKS WHEREVER BOOKS ARE SOLD, INCLUDING MOST BOOKSTORES, SUPERMARKETS, DISCOUNT STORES AND DRUGSTORES.

LICNM0323

HARLEQUIN
PLUS

Try the best multimedia subscription service for romance readers like you!

Read, Watch and Play.

Experience the easiest way to get the romance content you crave.

Start your **FREE TRIAL** at
www.harlequinplus.com/freetrial.